Classic Children's Stories

ARCTURUS

storytime

Text and illustrations copyright © 2017 Storytime Magazine
www.storytimemagazine.com

Illustration credits

Leo Antolini: *The Ant and the Grasshopper*; Marion Arbona: *The Rainbow Snake*;
Monica Armino: *Robin Hood and the Silver Arrow*; Sebastian Baculea: *Mouse Deer
and the Tiger*; Anni Betts: *How Rabbit Got Long Ears*; Marga Biazzi: *The Lucky
Pedlar*; Miriam Bos: *Bambi*; Brooke Boynton Hughes: *Goldilocks and the Three
Bears*; Alice Brereton: *The Blind Friends and the Elephant*; Princesse Camcam: *The
Wooden Bowl*; Rogério Coelho: *The Mouse Merchant*; Tel Coelho: *The Tortoise and
the Geese*; Lee Cosgrove: *The Farmer's Horse*; Juliana Cuervo: *The Wise Bear*;
Pippa Curnick: *The Fox and the Crow*; Aurore Damant: *The Gingerbread Man*;
Matt Dawson: *The Dog and his Bone*; Eléonore Della Malva: *Theseus and the
Minotaur*; David DePasquale: *Hans the Rabbit Herder*; Evelyne Duverne: *The Selkie
Wife*; Niña de Polonia: *Lazy Jack*; George Ermos: *The Boy Who Cried Wolf*;
Christina Forshay: *The Magic Harp*; Christelle Galloux: *Little Red Riding Hood*;
Justin Gerard: *St. George and the Dragon*; Anaïs Goldemberg: *The Polar Bear Son*;
Alexandra Huard: *Maui Goes Fishing*; Ines Huni: *The Three Sillies*;
Maria Karipidou: *Brer Rabbit*; Dan Kerleroux: *Three Billy Goats Gruff*;
Oliver Lake: *The Lion and the Mouse*; Kelly McLellan: *The Sword in the Stone*;
Victoria Maderna: *Stone Soup*; Teresa Martinez: *The Queen of Winter*;
Juana Martinez-Neal: *The Language of Birds*; Melanie Matthews: *Puss in Boots*,
Cover illustration; Sid Meireles: *Town Mouse and Country Mouse*;
Marisa Morea: *Cat and Mouse*; Karl James Mountford: *The Lost City of Atlantis*;
Chiara Nocentini: *Pinocchio*; Bruno Nunes: *Anansi the Spider*; Tim Paul: *Finn
MacCool*; Lucye Rioland: *The Four Dragons*; Sebastià Serra: *Sinbad's First Voyage*;
Corey R. Tabor: *The Four Harmonious Animals*, *The Hare and the Tortoise*;
Karl West: *Jack Seeks His Fortune*; Ryan Wheatcroft: *The Wise Folk of Gotham*;
Martin Wickstrom: *The Wish Fish*.

ARCTURUS

This edition published in 2017 by Arcturus Publishing Limited
26/27 Bickels Yard, 151–153 Bermondsey Street,
London SE1 3HA

Copyright © Arcturus Holdings Limited

ISBN: 978-1-78428-687-3
CH005640NT
Supplier 29, Date 0717, Print run 6237

Printed in China

Classic Children's Stories

Contents

Little Red Riding Hood 6

Goldilocks and the Three Bears 13

The Language of Birds 20

The Lion and the Mouse 26

Puss in Boots 29

Anansi the Spider 38

Sinbad's First Voyage 42

The Queen of Winter 48

The Lost City of Atlantis 52

The Rainbow Snake 56

The Hare and the Tortoise 59

Three Billy Goats Gruff 63

The Polar Bear Son 70

Brer Rabbit 74

Robin Hood and the Silver Arrow 80

Jack Seeks His Fortune 86

Bambi 91

Lazy Jack 99

The Tortoise and the Geese 104

Cat and Mouse 108

The Three Sillies 114

The Selkie Wife 120

Town Mouse and Country Mouse 126

The Blind Friends and the Elephant 130

The Wish Fish 133

Mouse Deer and the Tiger 138

The Sword in the Stone 144

The Lucky Pedlar 150

The Magic Harp 154

Maui Goes Fishing 160

How Rabbit Got Long Ears 164

The Ant and Grasshopper 169

The Gingerbread Man 173

The Mouse Merchant 180

The Four Dragons 184

The Wise Bear 190

Finn MacCool 193

Theseus and the Minotaur 198

The Boy Who Cried Wolf 204

The Farmer's Horse 208

St. George and the Dragon 212

The Dog and his Bone 216

The Four Harmonious Animals 220

Pinocchio 224

Stone Soup 231

The Wooden Bowl 235

Hans the Rabbit Herder 241

The Fox and the Crow 248

The Wise Folk of Gotham 252

Little Red Riding Hood

Once upon a time, there was a sweet little girl who was loved very much by all who knew her—but especially by her mother and her grandmother.

Her mother made her a red hooded cape to keep her warm, and she loved it so much that she wore it every day. Soon, she became known as Little Red Riding Hood. "Here comes Little Red Riding Hood!" the villagers would say.

"Hello, little girl," said the wolf.

One morning, her mother baked a cake and asked Little Red Riding Hood to take it to her grandmother, who lived in the woods.

"She isn't feeling well," said her mother, "and it will cheer her up to see you. Be as quick as you can, and please don't stray from the path."

Little Red Riding Hood kissed her mother goodbye and set out for the woods. As she walked along the woodland path, she spotted a clearing filled with pretty yellow flowers. "How lovely these will be for Grandmother!" thought Little Red Riding Hood, and she strayed from the path to take a closer look.

She had just started to pick a posy, when a great furry wolf stepped out from behind a tree. He had bright beady eyes and sharp white teeth.

"Hello, little girl," said the wolf. "Where are you heading on this fine morning?"

Little Red Riding Hood didn't know that wolves could be wicked, so she answered politely, "I am going to see my grandmother, who isn't very well."

"Does she live nearby?" asked the wolf.

"Just on the other side of the woods," said Little Red Riding Hood, "near the woodcutter's cottage, by the tall oak tree."

"I see," said the wolf, who was thinking up a plan. "Well, I'm sure that seeing you will make her feel much better. Good day, Little Red Riding Hood!"

"What a friendly wolf!" thought Little Red Riding Hood, and she continued picking flowers for her grandmother.

Meanwhile, the wolf bounded away through the trees as fast as he could, and he soon reached Grandmother's cottage. He knocked on the door, and she called out, "Who is it?"

"It's Little Red Riding Hood," the wolf said, trying hard to sound like a little girl. "I've brought you some flowers."

"Come in, my dear," said Grandmother. "The door is open."

The wicked wolf opened the door, bounded into the room, and ate up poor Grandmother in one big gulp!

Then, with a full belly, he slipped on Grandmother's nightgown, nightcap, and glasses, climbed into her bed, and pulled up the covers around him.

When Little Red Riding Hood arrived at the cottage, she knocked on the door and was surprised to hear a rough, gruff voice call out, "Who is it?"

"It's Little Red Riding Hood," she called, thinking that her grandmother must have a sore throat. "I have some cake and flowers to cheer you up!"

"Oh, come in, my dear," answered the wolf. "Just turn the handle—I am too tired to get up."

Little Red Riding Hood was surprised to see how very strange her grandmother looked. "What a terrible illness she must have!" she thought to herself.

"How lovely to see you, dear," said the wolf. "Now why don't you put down that heavy basket and come a little closer?"

Little Red Riding Hood stepped a little closer and said, "Grandmother, what big arms you have!"

"Why, all the better to hug you with, my dear!"

Little Red Riding Hood stepped closer yet and said, "Grandmother, what big ears you have!"

"All the better to hear you with, my dear!"

Little Red Riding Hood stepped even closer and said, "Grandmother, what big eyes you have!"

"All the better to see you with, my dear!"

Finally, Little Red Riding Hood stepped forward and said, "Grandmother, what big teeth you have!"

And with that, the wolf leaped out of Grandmother's bed and swallowed up Little Red Riding Hood in one great, greedy gulp! Poor Little Red Riding Hood!

By now, the wolf's stomach was about to burst, so he decided to lie down on the bed and take a nap. He began to snore so loudly that it shook the walls.

The woodcutter, who was on his way home, heard the snores and decided to check on Grandmother to see if she was feeling all right.

When he opened the door and saw the wolf asleep on the bed and Little Red Riding Hood's cape lying on the floor, he guessed that something terrible had happened.

"You scoundrel!" cried the woodcutter, and he took his hatchet and carefully cut open the wolf's big, fat belly.

As he did so, out jumped Little Red Riding Hood and out stepped her grandmother—they were both alive and very happy to be free again, and the wolf was dead!

Little Red Riding Hood and her grandmother thanked the woodcutter for saving their lives, then the three of them celebrated with a cup of tea and a slice of freshly baked cake—and Little Red Riding Hood vowed that she would never stray from the path again.

Goldilocks and the Three Bears

Once upon a time, there were three bears who lived in a sweet little cabin in the woods. The bears were great big Daddy Bear, medium-sized Mama Bear, and teeny little Baby Bear.

One morning, Daddy Bear made a delicious pot of porridge for their breakfast. He spooned it into their bowls—there was a teeny little bowl for Baby Bear, a medium-sized bowl for Mama Bear, and a great big bowl for Daddy Bear.

Goldilocks and the Three Bears

The porridge was too hot to eat, so the three bears decided to go for a quick walk in the woods while their breakfast cooled down.

While they were out walking, a little girl with a freckled nose and golden ringlets found their cabin. Her name was Goldilocks, and she lived on the other side of the woods. She was out picking blackberries for her mother.

She wondered who might live in the cabin, and when she peeped through the window, she saw three bowls of yummy porridge sitting on the table.

If Goldilocks had remembered her manners, she would have waited to be invited in. But curiosity got the better of her—and before she knew it, she had opened the front door and was standing by the breakfast table.

The porridge smelled so delicious, and Goldilocks was so hungry that her tummy began to rumble loudly. "Nobody will mind if I eat one little spoonful," she thought to herself.

So she ate a spoonful from the great big bowl, but it was too hot. She almost burned her lip!

Next, Goldilocks ate a spoonful of porridge from the medium-sized bowl, but it was too cold. "Yuck!" she cried, wishing she could spit it out again.

Still hungry, she ate
a spoonful of porridge
from the teeny little bowl,
and it was neither too hot
nor too cold—it was just
right. Goldilocks liked it
so much, she ate it all up!

Now Goldilocks was
feeling quite full, so she
decided to sit down.

She sat in a great big orange
chair, but it was too hard and
uncomfortable. She sat in a
medium-sized yellow chair, but
it was too soft and deep.

Finally, Goldilocks sat in a teeny little
blue chair, and it was neither too hard
nor too soft—it was just right. But then
the seat snapped in half, and she fell
to the floor with a bump. Oh dear!

By now, Goldilocks was feeling very
tired, and she wanted to lie down. In
the bedroom, she found three beds.

First, she tried to lie on the great big
bed, but it was too high up for her.
Next, she lay on the medium-sized
bed, but it was too low and saggy.

Then, she lay on the teeny little bed,
and it was neither too high nor too
low—it was just right. So she crept
under the comfy blankets and soon
drifted off to sleep.

The three bears thought that their
porridge must have cooled down, so
they wandered home for breakfast.
But when they got there, Daddy Bear
noticed that his spoon was standing
in his great big bowl of porridge.

boomed Daddy Bear in his great big voice!

Mama Bear saw that the table around her bowl was very messy.

"Who's been eating my porridge?" she asked in her medium-sized voice.

Then Baby Bear found that his teeny little bowl was completely empty!

"Who's been eating my porridge—and they've eaten it all up!" he cried in his teeny little voice.

The three bears started to look around the cabin for clues. Daddy Bear noticed that the great big cushion on his great big chair had moved.

"Who's been sitting in my chair?" he boomed in his great big voice.

Mama Bear saw that the medium-sized cushion on her medium-sized chair had a small dent in it.

"Who's been sitting in my chair?" she asked in her medium-sized voice.

Meanwhile, Baby Bear was standing by his very own teeny little chair and looking very sad.

"Who's been sitting in my chair—and they've broken it in half!" he cried in his teeny little voice.

The three bears decided to check their bedroom. When they opened the door, Daddy Bear noticed that the covers had been pulled off his great big bed.

"Who's been sleeping in my bed?" he boomed in his great big voice.

The three bears decided to check their bedroom.

Mama Bear saw that the pillows on her medium-sized bed had moved.

"Who's been sleeping in my bed?" she asked in her medium-sized voice.

Then, Baby Bear looked at his teeny little bed and saw that there was a little girl with a freckled nose and golden ringlets lying in it—and she was fast asleep!

"Who's been sleeping in my bed—and she's still in it!" he cried in his teeny little voice.

Naughty Goldilocks woke up, jumped at the sight of the three bears, tumbled out of the bed, and dashed out of the cabin. Then she ran and ran as fast as her legs could carry her, completely forgetting the blackberries she had picked!

The three bears never saw Goldilocks again, but it's a shame that she ran away, because teeny little Baby Bear had been hoping to make a new friend that day.

The Language of Birds

Long ago in Russia, there was a boy named Ivan, who was the son of a rich merchant. For all Ivan's good fortune, he longed with all his heart to understand the language of birds.

Ivan owned a caged nightingale, and every evening after dinner, he would listen to the bird's sweet song and long to know what it meant.

One day, he went hunting in the forest, and the wind suddenly started to whip around him. The rain lashed down, and the thunder rumbled. Ivan ran to shelter under a large tree and noticed a nest with four baby birds in its branches.

Worried about the chicks, he decided to climb the tree and drape his cloak over their nest to protect them.

Eventually, the thunderstorm passed, and the chick's mother—a beautiful owl—returned to the nest. When she saw what Ivan had done, she spoke to him in a clear voice: "Thank you for protecting my children, kind sir. What can I give you in return?"

"I have a good life," said Ivan, "but there is one thing I wish for. Can you teach me the language of birds?"

The mother owl agreed. "Stay here with me for three days, and I will teach you all I can," she said.

Ivan stayed in the forest. At the end of three days, he understood the language of birds. He set out for home, excited by his new gift.

That evening, after dinner with his parents, Ivan's nightingale began to sing, and he listened attentively. Soon, he started to weep.

"What is wrong, son?" asked his father.

"It's so terribly sad!" said Ivan, and tears rolled down his cheeks.

"What has happened?" demanded his father, who was starting to feel frightened by his son's crying.

"Oh, Father," explained Ivan, "when I was in the forest, I learned the language of birds. Now I understand my nightingale's song. It is so sad."

"You are scaring us, Ivan! What did it sing?" cried his mother.

"The nightingale sang that one day I will no longer be your son, and you, Father, will be my servant."

"Nonsense!" said his father. However, that night, he couldn't sleep because he was so troubled by what Ivan had heard.

Over the following days, Ivan sat for hours listening to his nightingale, and slowly, his parents started to believe that he would betray them in some way and steal their fortune.

One night, when Ivan was sleeping soundly, his father carried him to the port, placed him in a small boat, and pushed him out to sea.

By the time Ivan awoke, he was far from land, and he spent a desperate night bobbing on the waves, until the sailors of a passing ship spotted his boat and helped him aboard.

Soon after Ivan boarded the ship, some seabirds flew overhead, and Ivan heard them speaking of an approaching storm. He rushed to warn the ship's captain.

"Captain, the birds say there will be a terrible storm tonight. I think you should enter the nearest port."

The captain laughed at Ivan, and all the other sailors joined in—but that night, there came a storm that lashed and tore at the sails, tearing them to pieces. It took days to repair the ship.

A week later, Ivan saw some wild swans flying by, chatting noisily to each other. This time, the captain asked Ivan what they said.

"There is a notorious band of pirates nearby," said Ivan. "They plan to rob any ships that pass by. I think we should find a safe port."

This time, the crew listened to Ivan and made haste to the nearest port. From there, they saw the pirates attack many merchant ships.

The captain thanked Ivan and invited him to stay aboard. Ivan agreed, and they set off across the seas.

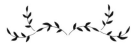

Before long, they dropped anchor in the main port of a country that was ruled by a wealthy king.

Word quickly reached the ship that the king was being plagued by three noisy crows. They were constantly squawking by the window of his bedchamber and wouldn't go away.

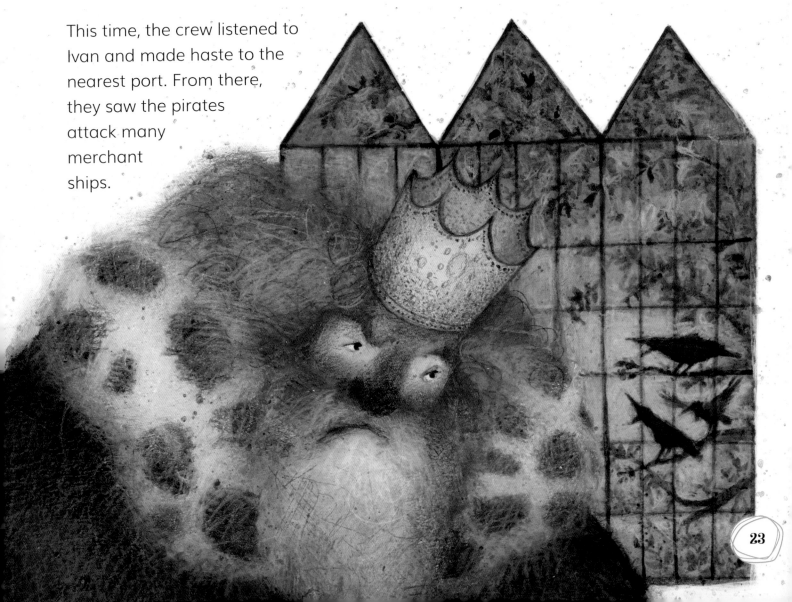

The king was so desperate for a peaceful night's sleep that, on his orders, his guards had posted notices all over town declaring that whoever could rid him of the crows would win his youngest daughter's hand in marriage. However, anyone who failed would have his head cut off!

Ivan hoped that his knowledge of the language of birds would bring him luck, and he headed for the palace. When he got there, he was escorted to the king's bedchamber, where he asked a servant to open the windows. The servants were quite puzzled to see Ivan sit down and do nothing. After a while, he asked the servants to take him to the king.

Ivan found the king seated on his throne looking drained and tired. He bowed before him.

"Sire, I speak the language of birds, and the three crows at your window are mother, father, and son. They are arguing about whether the son should follow his mother or father in life. They want you to decide."

Wearily and with great doubt at Ivan's ability, the king yawned and said, "The son should follow his father."

Ivan conveyed the king's message to the crows. Immediately, they flew away, never to be seen again! The exhausted king was so overjoyed that he married Ivan to the princess and gave him half his kingdom, too.

While all this had been happening, far away, Ivan's mother had died from old age, and his father felt so guilty at the way he had treated his son that he gave up work. He gradually lost his fortune and his home, and he was forced to travel from one town to the next, begging for food and shelter.

One day, his travels led him to the door of Ivan's palace, and when Ivan saw him, he knew immediately that it was his father. However, Ivan's father didn't know his son, since he was dressed in all his royal finery.

"What can I do for you, old man?" Ivan enquired.

"If you are good enough, sir, I would happily work as your faithful and humble servant in exchange for some food and shelter," said the old man.

"Oh, Father!" smiled Ivan. "Don't you know your own son? It seems that the nightingale's song turned out to be true, after all!"

Ivan's father then knew that he was looking at his son. Suddenly, all his grief vanished. He threw his arms around Ivan and begged for his forgiveness.

The old man did not become his son's servant, of course—Ivan's heart was far too kind. Instead, he forgave his father and made sure that he lived his last years in great comfort—and in the company of a caged nightingale.

The Lion and the Mouse

It was a hot, dry day in the forest—a lazy type of day where you just want to stretch out long and yawn. This was just what the lion was doing when a little mouse came scampering toward him.

She was on her way home, but the sun's rays were shining so brightly in her eyes that she didn't see the lion in the clearing ahead of her. Before she knew it, she was running up his leg, along his back, through his majestic golden mane, and all the way to the tip of his long lion nose.

The snoozing lion was annoyed to be disturbed by the ticklish pitter-patter of the mouse's feet, so he swiped his great paw at his nose and grabbed the mouse in his long, sharp claws.

"Who dares to walk over me—the King of the Jungle?" growled the hot and bothered lion.

He was just about to open his huge jaws and swallow the mouse whole, when he heard her squeak in a trembling voice, "Oh please, mighty lion, please let me go. My children are waiting for me at home. If you let me live now, then one day, I may be able to repay your kindness. Perhaps I will be able to help you?"

With that, the lion roared loudly—not with anger, but with laughter.

"You! A little mouse like you helping me ... the strongest and fiercest animal in the land? That's the funniest thing I've ever heard!"

The lion was so amused at the idea, he loosened his grip on the mouse, and she escaped. She ran and ran as fast as she could, all the way home.

Later that week, some hunters visited the forest and left behind a big trap.

They wanted to impress the leader of their tribe by capturing the lion for him. The lion didn't see the trap. While proudly prowling through the undergrowth, swishing his long tail, he walked straight into a net of ropes and became entangled in it.

The lion roared and thrashed and clawed and lashed that tail of his, but he couldn't break free. He just became more and more tied up. In frustration, he let out a roar so loud that it shook the forest floor.

The little mouse heard the lion's desperate cry and scurried off in its direction. When she arrived, she saw the lion entwined in the net. His magnificent mane was flat against his head, and his eyes were closed.

Quickly—before the hunters returned—the mouse used her sharp teeth to nibble at a thick rope until it snapped in two. Then she nibbled another and another, until all the ropes came loose. The lion opened his eyes and was surprised to see the mouse gnawing on a rope near his paws.

"I was wrong," growled the lion, as he shook away the last few ropes. "I should never have laughed at you. Even though you are small, you have helped me, just as you said you would. Thank you, dear mouse."

And from that day on, the lion and the mouse became great friends, and the lion never again doubted the strength, wit, or bravery of his little companion.

Puss in Boots

Once upon a time, a poor miller died, leaving his three sons only a mill, a donkey, and a cat between them.

The eldest brother took charge of the inheritance and gave himself the mill, the donkey went to the middle brother, and the youngest brother got the cat.

The brothers went their separate ways, and the younger one moaned, "Oh, it's all very well for them—they can make a fine living with a mill and a donkey, but what am I to do with this cat? Even if I eat it and use its fur to make a hat, I'll still starve in the long run."

The cat heard every word the brother said, and alarmed at the thought of being his dinner, it said, "Don't worry, master. Give me a bag and a pair of boots and I promise that I will help improve your fortunes."

The brother was taken aback by his talking cat. However, he had seen him show great cunning when catching mice, so he spent his last few pennies on the items the cat had asked for.

Later that day, the cat slung his new bag over his shoulder, pulled on his new boots, and purred with delight. Then he put some vegetables in the bag and said, "Leave things to me, master." And off he strolled to the nearest meadow.

The brother watched the cat open the bag, then lie down next to it and play dead. Before long, two large rabbits hopped up to the bag, sniffed at it, and crawled inside. The cat leaped up and closed the bag with the rabbits still in it.

He gave one rabbit to the brother, then set off for the palace, where he asked to see the king. Impressed by Puss in Boots, the guards led him to the king's private quarters, where the cat bowed low to the king and announced, "Your Majesty, I present to you a fine rabbit from my noble Master of Carabas."

Amused by the sight of this cat in boots, the king said, "You may tell your master that I am most thankful."

The next day, the cat returned to the meadow with his bag filled with grain. He played dead next to the bag and a pair of fat pheasants waddled into it. Again, he gave one pheasant to his master and presented the other to the king as a gift from his master.
This went on for a couple of months, until everyone at the palace got to know Puss in Boots well—and the king started to wonder who was this most generous Master of Carabas.

On one visit to the palace, Puss in Boots discovered that the king and his daughter would be taking a long drive along the river the next day.

The cat darted home and said, "Tomorrow, master, you must bathe in the river. Do as I say, and your fortune will be made!"

The next day, the brother did as the cat told him and was bathing in the river, when he spotted the king's carriage approaching. He heard Puss in Boots cry, "Help! Help! The Master of Carabas is drowning!"

When the king saw Puss in Boots, he commanded his guards to pull over and help. As they dragged the brother from the river, the cat explained that a group of fiendish bandits had robbed his master of his clothes and thrown him in the river.

The king instructed his guards to fetch a fine suit for the Master of Carabas. Soon, the brother looked just like a noble lord. In fact, he looked so regal, the princess fell in love with him.

Intrigued to meet the man who had sent him so many generous gifts, the king invited the Master of Carabas to ride with them in his carriage. Puss in Boots winked, so the brother knew to play along with it.

As he chatted with the king and the princess, Puss in Boots ran on ahead.

He soon met some farmers mowing a field. "The king is coming," the cat said. "When he asks who this field belongs to, you must tell him it is owned by the Master of Carabas—or you will be put to death!"

So when the king passed by and asked who owned the field, the frightened farmers all chimed, "The Master of Carabas, Your Majesty."

The brother smiled at Puss in Boots' cleverness and said, "Yes, this field always gives me a plentiful harvest."

Puss in Boots ran on ahead again to a field of reapers. "When the king comes by," he warned them, "you must tell him that this field belongs to the Master of Carabas—or you will be put to death!"

So when the king reached the field and asked who owned it, the reapers answered without hesitation, "The Master of Carabas, Your Majesty."

The king congratulated the brother on such a fine harvest, and the brother nodded and smiled with much pleasure.

And so this went on. As the journey continued, the cat ran ahead to make sure that every worker they passed claimed to work for the Master of Carabas. The king, of course, was hugely impressed.

Puss in Boots ran on ahead until he reached a grand castle. This castle was owned by a rich but cruel ogre, who had the power to change into any shape he liked—and Puss knew very well that all the land the king had passed through belonged to this ogre.

Puss in Boots asked the castle guards if he might have the privilege of paying his respects to the great ogre. Deeply flattered to receive such a message—for the ogre was terribly vain—he welcomed the cat into his throne room and invited him to take a seat.

The cat flattered the ogre with many compliments, then said, "I have heard that you can change into any creature you wish, but I find it hard to believe. I have heard, for instance, that you can change into an elephant or a lion."

"It is true!" boasted the ogre. "I can show you my powers right now!" And in an instant, he changed into a lion and let out a mighty roar.

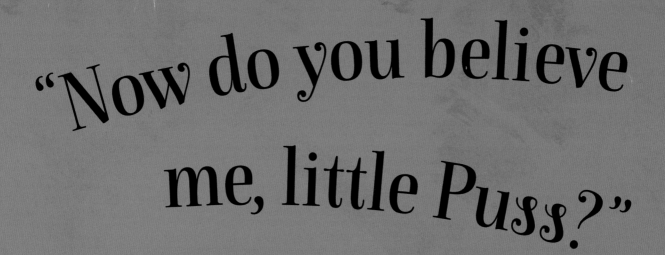

"Now do you believe me, little Puss?"

The cat was truly terrified and jumped onto the table, his fur standing on end. The ogre changed back into his normal shape and laughed at the cat.

"Impressive!" said Puss in Boots, trying to calm himself. "But an ogre of your size must find it impossible to change into a small animal, like a mouse."

"Impossible?" said the ogre. "I don't think so!" And in a flash, he turned into a tiny mouse and scurried across the floor. Wasting no time, Puss in Boots leaped on the mouse and killed it, putting an end to the ogre forever.

Just then, the king's carriage pulled up outside the castle. Impressed by its size and grandeur, the king decided to pay its owner a visit.

When the cat heard the carriage on the drawbridge, he dashed outside to greet the king and princess.

"We are delighted to welcome you to the home of my Master of Carabas!"

The king was astonished, as was the brother, who did his best to hide his surprise. Still pretending he was the Master of Carabas, he smiled at the king and led the princess into the great hall, where a magnificent feast lay before them. The feast was the ogre's lunch, but as the ogre was no more, they dined together in style.

By the end of their feast, the king was so charmed by the Master of Carabas, he suggested that he should marry the princess. The brother and the princess both thought this was a wonderful idea.

After their wedding, they made the ogre's castle their home, and Puss in Boots spent his days curled up on a velvet cushion, lapping up saucers of cream. His promise fulfilled, the clever cat never again did a day's work.

Anansi the Spider

Anansi the spider's mouth was watering. He had picked some fat, juicy yams from his garden, and they were baking slowly on the fire. Oh, they smelled so good!

Anansi was setting the table when he spied his friend Turtle through the window. He was climbing up the steep hill toward the spider's house. "Oh no!" thought Anansi. "I wanted these delicious yams all to myself. I don't want to share!" Then he quickly closed the curtains to make it look as if nobody was home.

KNOCK

KNOCK

But just as Anansi sat down to eat, there was a slow knock on his door. It was Turtle, and he looked very tired and hungry.

"Anansi, I have walked all day, and my feet are sore and aching. Please will you share some of your delicious-smelling yams with me?"

Now, where Anansi lived, it was customary to share your meal with a guest, however unexpected they were. So Anansi couldn't say no.

"Of course! Please take a seat, Turtle," said Anansi, and he laid the table, all the time trying to decide how to get rid of his unwanted guest.

Just as Turtle was reaching for a fat, juicy yam, Anansi cried, "Goodness me, Turtle! Look at you! We don't eat with dirty hands in my house—please go and wash them in the river!"

Turtle's hands were indeed very dirty, as he'd been walking all day, so he left the table and ambled down to the river to get himself clean.

By the time he got back, Anansi had eaten one of the yams already. "I thought I should start before they get too cold," Anansi said slyly.

Turtle reached for a yam again, but Anansi wailed, "Turtle! Your hands are still so dirty! Please, you must wash them properly!"

Of course, Turtle's hands became dirty walking back from the river, so this time he washed very thoroughly and crawled back over the grass to avoid getting dusty again.

But while he was gone, greedy Anansi gobbled up the yams as quickly as he could. When Turtle got back to Anansi's house, he stood in the doorway and sighed a hungry sigh. Poor Turtle hadn't even tasted a mouthful!

"Well, thank you for letting me be your guest, Anansi. Please let me return the kindness one day. You must come to my house for dinner soon."

Turtle trundled away, and Anansi slapped his full belly and thought, "What a good trick that was!"

A few days later, Anansi decided to take Turtle up on his offer. Anansi loved eating—especially when somebody else had cooked the food!

He put on his most stylish jacket and set off on the long journey up the river to Turtle's house. When he arrived, he was hot, tired, hungry, and thirsty—and he could not stop thinking of the delicious morsels he might eat.

Turtle was lying on a rock in the late afternoon sunshine. "Hello, Anansi! You look tired. Have you come over for dinner?"

"Oh yes, please!" said Anansi, whose tummy was starting to growl.

"I'll just lay the table," said Turtle, and he dived down into the river to his underwater home. He was gone for a short time, then he popped up again.

"Okay, dinner is ready now. Please dive down and join me."

Anansi was a little surprised to be having an underwater dinner, but he was so hungry, he didn't care.

At the bottom of the river, he could just make out a table laden with tasty treats. Anansi eagerly jumped in and tried to dive to the bottom, but however hard he swam, he just kept bobbing up to the top.

Turtle smiled and waved up at him from the bottom of the river—he had already started eating.

Anxious not to miss a free meal, Anansi came up with a plan—he stuffed his pockets with heavy rocks, and this time, he sank right down to Turtle's table and stayed there!

Anansi couldn't wait to get started— Turtle had laid out a fantastic feast! However, just as he went to eat his first mouthful, Turtle cried, "Goodness me, Anansi! Look at you! We don't wear jackets at the dinner table here—please take it off!"

It was true; Turtle wasn't wearing a jacket. Not wishing to be rude, Anansi did as Turtle asked. However, as soon as he took off his jacket, without the rocks to weigh him down, he floated straight up to the surface of the river.

With a grumbling tummy, Anansi stuck his head under the water and watched Turtle slowly finish his delicious meal.

Turtle had certainly returned the kindness!

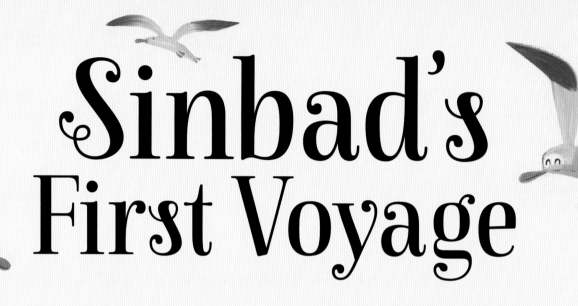

Sinbad's First Voyage

L ong ago in Baghdad, there lived a hard-working porter named
Sinbad. He earned a scanty living lugging things around for
people, and the money he had in his pocket was never quite enough.

One blistering hot day, he was carrying a particularly heavy load and needed to
rest. He sat down outside the home of a wealthy merchant. As he sat there, he
heard music and happy voices drifting through the window. He peeked inside and
saw a beautiful garden with a fountain and servants bringing out a feast.

"How is it," cried Sinbad in despair, "that I slave so hard all the hours of the day,
yet I will never see a life of comfort like this?"

His heart ached with the unfairness of it all. He lifted up his heavy load to continue his journey, but as he did so, a servant appeared at the gate.

"Sir, my master wishes to see you."

The porter was puzzled as he had never met the owner of the house, but he followed the servant through the gates into a garden overflowing with fruit trees, fountains, and flowers. Sinbad the porter thought that he must be in paradise.

Seated on a silk cushion, surrounded by his friends and courtiers, was a nobleman dressed in fine clothes. The porter bowed, but the nobleman told him to stand up and invited him to eat as much as he liked.

Sinbad was delighted by his good fortune. He ate until he was full and thanked his host. The nobleman said, "You are welcome, hard-working stranger," for he had heard Sinbad's cries outside the gate. "Now tell me your name, sir."

"I am Sinbad the porter."

The host's face broke into a grin, and he said, "Well, we have something in common. I, too, am Sinbad—Sinbad the sailor—and I was once a poor, hard-working man like you. Take a seat, and I will tell you my tale."

So Sinbad the porter made himself comfortable, and Sinbad the sailor began his story.

"My father was a wealthy merchant, and I grew up without a worry in the world. But I was a foolish young man and quickly wasted the money he had worked so hard for all his life.

"When there was nothing left, I was forced to sell my family home, my possessions, and even my clothes.

"With the money I had left, I hired a ship and a crew, and went to seek adventure at sea. We set off for the nearest big port, and over the next few months, we traded whatever we could, increasing our wealth at each place we dropped anchor.

"One day, we came to a beautiful island covered in exotic plants and trees. It had sand so golden that it sparkled in the sunlight. Eager to feel the sand on our bare feet, we ran ashore. Only the captain stayed on board. We spent the afternoon lazing on the beach, and when the sun began to set, we lit campfires. Within moments, we heard the ship's bell ringing and the captain shouting, 'Run for your lives!'

"At once, the beach began to shudder violently, throwing us off our feet. We ran as quickly as we could toward the ship, but towering waves started to crash against the shore. The island lifted into the air and tipped to one side, forcing many of my crew to slide into the churning sea below.

"As I fell with them, I grabbed the trunk of a falling palm tree. It was this that saved my life, and I gripped it tightly as the waves tossed me back and forth. Eventually, I managed to climb onto the trunk. When I looked up, I saw that the beautiful island we had moored at was no island at all—it was a beast of a whale, much bigger than any I have ever seen before or since. Our fires must have woken it from its deep slumber.

"The angry whale thrashed its tail and dived down, creating an enormous wave that swept me far from my ship. By now, night had fallen, and with the ship far in the distance, I felt that I was sure to meet my doom.

"All I could do was cling to the tree trunk and hope for survival. But luck was on my side. As dawn broke, I washed up on the sandy shore of an unknown place.

"As soon as I had recovered, I walked along the beach. In the distance, I noted a majestic-looking mare, roped to a tree. As I approached, a great blue horse emerged from the sea—a ghostly sea-stallion—and started to drag the mare into the sea, where she would surely drown. I couldn't stand by and watch, so I grabbed a stick and ran toward the sea-stallion, fighting it off furiously.

"The mare neighed with terror, but at last, the supernatural beast gave up and galloped back into the waves. As I calmed the mare, a groom came running over.

"'I must thank you, kind stranger,' he said. 'You have just saved the life of King Mirjan's best-loved horse.'

"The groom invited me to travel with him to the capital city, and when we arrived, he told King Mirjan what had happened. The king insisted on thanking me personally. When I told him the tale of my first voyage, he was convinced that I must be blessed. 'Any other man would have drowned 500 times!' he laughed.

"He offered me a job as master of the island's main port, where each day I registered all the ships that came in and out. Imagine my joy when, one day, my own ship came into port! The captain knew me at once and hauled out a chest with all the money I had made on our voyage together—it had survived the attack of the monstrous island whale.

"I took the chest to King Mirjan to thank him for his kindness. In return, he rewarded me with a casket bursting with jewels!

"I said farewell to him, then sailed with my crew to a large city port, where I sold the jewels for ten times the value of my chest. I was rich! By the time I returned to Baghdad, my first voyage had made me wealthy enough to buy this palace and all the comforts we are enjoying today."

Sinbad the sailor ended the tale of his exciting adventures by giving the porter a bag filled with 100 gold coins. And Sinbad the porter delivered his heavy load, wondering if his own life might now begin to have the same good fortune as Sinbad the sailor's.

The Queen of Winter

Long ago, when the world was young, Scotland was ruled over by a powerful goddess named Cailleach, who sat on a throne at the top of Ben Nevis.

Cailleach roamed the mountains and glens of Scotland, guarding the wolves, deer, and cattle from hunters. Everywhere she went, she was followed by the wild animals who loved her. She wore an old shawl and always carried her magic hammer. With these two things, she reigned supreme as the Queen of Winter.

Every year in late autumn, she washed her shawl in the sea and placed it on top of the mountains to dry. When she lifted it, the peaks were covered with snow. Then, using the hills as stepping stones, she journeyed across the land, pounding it with her magic hammer to spread frost and ice in all directions.

As winter went on, with each passing day, Cailleach grew older. Her brow became wrinkled, and her hair turned white and trailed behind her. At the end of every winter, she journeyed to sip from the secret Well of Youth, then she slept through spring and summer.

However, one year, Cailleach decided that she wanted winter to last forever. She covered Scotland with a heavy blanket of snow, stirred up biting gales, and froze the rivers and lochs solid. Soon everyone wished for spring.

Cailleach had many servants, and one of them was a fair young lady called Bride. Bride had golden-brown hair and eyes like violets.

Cailleach had always been jealous of Bride's youth and beauty—so she always gave her the most horrible chores to do. One day, she sent Bride down to the icy river and told her to wash a brown wool blanket until it was pure white. It was an impossible task. After scrubbing for many hours, Bride's hands were so blue with the cold, she broke down and wept.

But as her tears fell to the icy ground, snowdrops suddenly pushed their tiny, delicate heads through the snow. And when she stood up to make her way back to Cailleach, primroses sprang up at her feet. You see, the Queen of Winter didn't know that many years before, the fairies had blessed young Bride with the spirit of spring.

Bride's path passed by a mountain where Cailleach's son, blue-eyed Angus, lived. When Angus saw Bride and the flowers springing up around her every step, he was so moved that he fell in love with her.

Angus rushed out to speak to Bride. As he did so, grass grew around their feet, and a bird broke the wintry silence with its sweet song. The magic of spring was happening all around them. Bride's heart was filled with joy, because she knew that Cailleach's frosty reign must be coming to an end —and that she and Angus were meant to rule over spring together.

When Cailleach saw the snow melting, she was filled with fury. Though she felt worn and frail, she smashed her magic hammer to the ground, so that no flower could bloom and no blade of grass could survive. She caused a violent snowstorm to whip around Bride and Angus, which tore the new flowers from their stalks.

However, the strength of their love soon weakened Cailleach's powers—spring was surging through the land, and there was nothing the Queen of Winter could do to fight it. She had run out of strength.

Knowing that her reign was over, Cailleach fled to the Well of Youth, where she took a sip from its magic waters and became young and beautiful again. There, she fell into a deep slumber that lasted until the following winter.

Meanwhile, Bride dipped her hand into the river, and the ice melted away. The fish jumped in celebration, the birds burst into song, and together, she and Angus walked the land, bringing it back to life. The Queen and King of Spring had chased the Queen of Winter away ... for now.

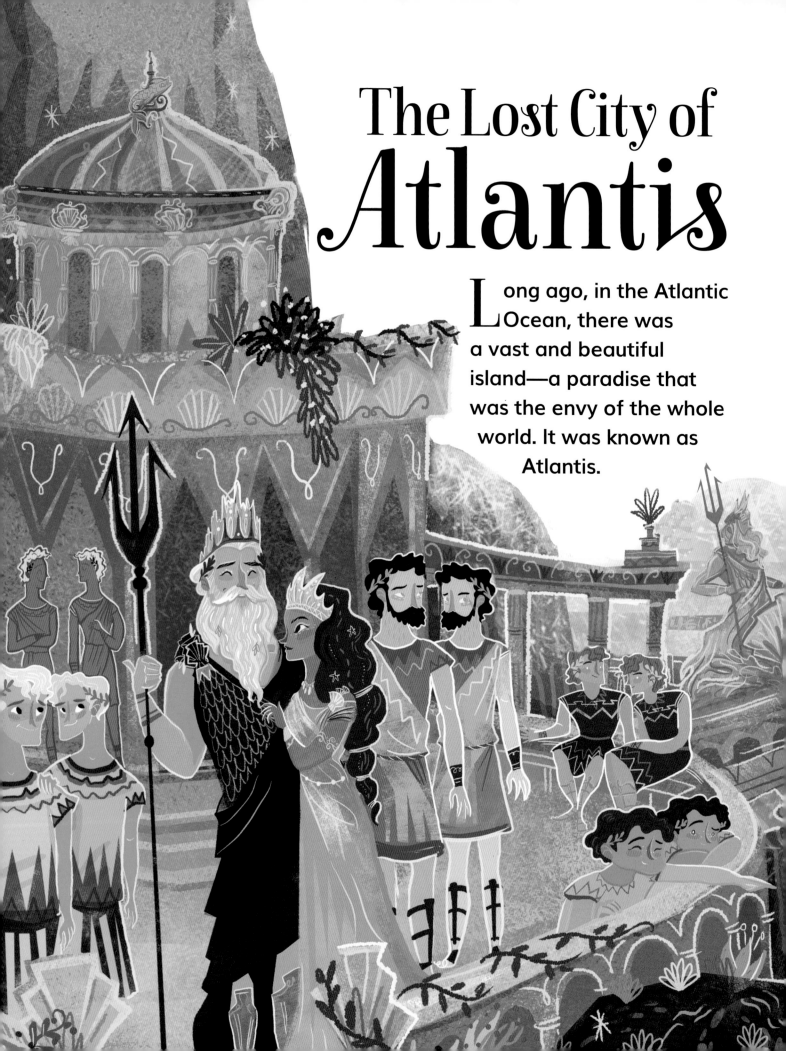

The Lost City of
Atlantis

Long ago, in the Atlantic Ocean, there was a vast and beautiful island—a paradise that was the envy of the whole world. It was known as Atlantis.

At first, Atlantis was ruled over by Poseidon, who was the god of the sea. When he fell in love with a mortal woman named Cleito, he built a grand palace for her on top of a mountain in the middle of the island. Then he surrounded it with three great rings of water to protect her. These rings also ensured that the island remained forever rich and fertile.

Poseidon and Cleito were very happy together, and they had five sets of twin boys. As soon as he was old enough, the eldest of the ten sons, Atlas, was crowned the king of Atlantis, freeing Poseidon to rule over the sea.

He lived in the mountaintop palace with his mother, Cleito, and created a stunning temple with a golden statue of Poseidon, so that people could come and pray to his father.

He also built a magnificent city with marble walls and ornate bridges over the rings of water. Then he gave his nine brothers their own island territories to rule over. Together the ten sons worked hard to make sure that Atlantis was a peaceful and prosperous place. The great island's many orchards hung heavy with fruit, its mines were laden with precious metals and stones, and its forests, rivers, plains, and hills were

teeming with meat and fish to hunt. The people of Atlantis thought themselves the luckiest people in the world—and they were the subject of great envy, far and wide.

When Atlas and his brothers died, Poseidon decided that Atlantis should be governed by ten kings. Each king had to swear an oath that they would follow the rules of the gods and worship at Poseidon's temple. As long as the rulers followed Poseidon's laws,

Atlantis would thrive and prosper. But if they ignored these rules, Poseidon warned that Atlantis would suffer.

◆◆

It wasn't long before the new rulers of Atlantis started to behave foolishly. Taking their wealth for granted and feeling greedy for more power, they began to ignore their duties on the island, and made plans to invade and rule other countries. They stopped visiting the temple of Poseidon and neglected the land and their people. Without great leaders to inspire them, the people of Atlantis grew lazy. They let their farmland grow wild and didn't care for their animals. They began to raid other countries, such as Greece and Egypt, to steal their riches. They became so obsessed with power, that they set out to conquer the world and wreaked misery wherever they went.

When Poseidon witnessed what was happening to his beloved Atlantis, he journeyed to Mount Olympus and called a meeting with the gods.

Zeus, who was the most powerful god of all, was so angered by the humans' greedy conduct that he decided to teach them an important lesson. He conjured up a violent earthquake and flood, which, in one night, swallowed the isle of Atlantis and all who lived there. As the island sank into the depths of the sea, Poseidon shed tears of heavy sorrow.

The once-great nation of Atlantis was no more, but it has never been forgotten. Even today, intrepid explorers still search for this secret sunken island under the sea.

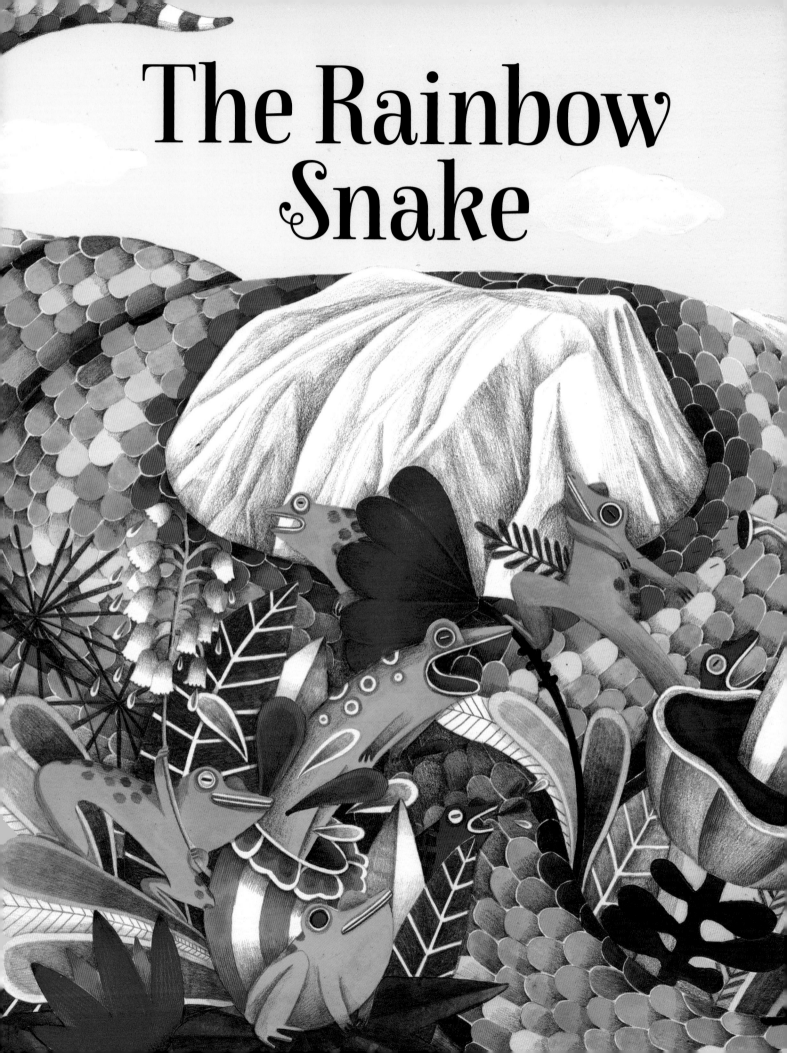

The Rainbow Snake

At the dawn of time, Australia was completely flat. There were no mountains or valleys, no rivers or lakes—just level plains as far as the eye could see. There were no birds in the sky, no fish in the sea, and no animals running across these plains. Everything was bare and silent and dull.

But one day, a great Rainbow Snake pushed its way out from beneath the earth and slithered and wound its way across the land. As it did so, its body gouged out great gorges, valleys, and craters, pushing the land up on either side to make hills, ridges, and craggy mountains. At the end of the day, the Rainbow Snake was tired, and it fell asleep in a large coil. When it woke up in the morning, there in the middle of the snake's coil was a beautiful red rock, which became known as Uluru, or Ayers Rock.

After it had finished shaping the landscape, the Rainbow Snake soon got bored and decided to bring life to the world it had created. So, it spat out some frogs, and it tickled their bellies with its forked tongue. The frogs giggled and laughed, and as they did so, water flowed out from their mouths, filling up the gorges to make fast-flowing rivers and flooding inside the craters to make waterholes and lakes.

Once there was water, many plants and trees quickly sprang to life, and the Rainbow Snake called to the animals to wake them up, too. Soon, everything was alive with movement and shapes and noise.

When the Rainbow Snake's work was complete, it slithered away to rest in the deepest waterhole.

It still sleeps there today, and the only time it is ever seen is when the rain pounds heavily on the surface of the waterhole. Then, the Rainbow Snake lifts its huge, brilliant body upward, arching it across the sky from one waterhole to the next,

just like a rainbow.

The Hare and the Tortoise

Hare was a boastful animal—always showing off about how tremendously fast he was at running.

"You know, I have never yet been beaten," he bragged to the animals who were gathered in the woodland clearing. He proudly puffed out his chest. "In fact, when I'm going at full speed, I am simply unbeatable!"

Fox rolled his eyes, and Hedgehog shook his head. They had heard Hare show off like this many times before. "If you don't believe me," Hare said, "I can prove it to you! I challenge anyone here to race me!"

Everyone in the clearing was quiet, until a little voice piped up: "I accept your challenge." It was Tortoise.

"Ha!" snorted Hare. "That's a good joke! Why, I could dance around you the whole way, and I'd win the race! I could hop backward on one leg, and you'd still lose! There is no animal in the forest slower than you, dear Tortoise!" Hare slapped his thigh and chortled to himself.

"Well, why not save your boasting until you've won?" said Tortoise. "Would you like to race me or not?" Hare looked at Tortoise in disbelief —but he was being totally serious!

"Well," thought Hare, "why not make this slow creature look like a fool? At least I can show everyone how very fast and brilliant I am!"

Hare agreed to race with Tortoise. The pair decided that Fox would set the course and start the race, and Hedgehog would wait at the finish line to declare the winner.

On the day of the race, Hare and Tortoise both stood at the starting line. All the forest animals gathered to watch. They wondered whether Tortoise might have a special trick to help him win the race.

When Fox waved to start the race, Hare bounded away as fast as he could, which was very fast indeed. He hadn't gone far when he noticed that Tortoise was nowhere to be seen. He looked back to find Tortoise moving at his usual leisurely pace.

"Why, this is no race at all!" thought Hare. "Look at him plodding along like that. I'll show him how it's done!"

So Hare went even faster—faster than he had ever raced before. He was so speedy, in fact, that when he reached the halfway point in the course on the other side of the hill, he felt very much out of breath.

"Hmm, why don't I have a little rest?" Hare thought. "After all, Tortoise is probably still near the starting line! Ha! I'm so fast, I could have a quick nap and still win the race!" So Hare found a nice, tufty patch of grass, curled up, and went to sleep.

Tortoise, meanwhile, continued plodding along, slow and steady, with a knowing little smile on his face. He didn't stop for a break even once.

He just kept on going ... plod, plod, plodding along ... all the way over the hill and straight past Hare, who was still snoozing.

It was only the sound of Hedgehog, Fox, and all the other animals cheering loudly that made Hare wake up with a jolt. Confused, he leapt to his feet, got back on the racecourse, and dashed at full speed toward the finish.

But as he turned the corner, what did he see, but Tortoise slowly plodding across the finish line? There was no way Hare could catch up with him now! Gasping for breath, Hare threw himself over the line, but it was too late. While Hare had been dozing, Tortoise—the slowest animal in the forest—had beaten him. That day, Hare learned a very important lesson ...

Slow and steady wins the race!

Three Billy Goats Gruff

Once upon a time, there were three billy goat brothers who lived in a beautiful valley in the mountains. There was Little Billy Goat Gruff, Medium Billy Goat Gruff, and Big Billy Goat Gruff.

The three goats were always hungry and loved to gnaw all day on fresh green grass, but they had eaten so much of it that their side of the valley had become bare and dry. One day, they stood looking longingly at the green fields on the other side of the valley and decided to live there instead.

However, there was only one way to reach the other side of the valley, and that was by crossing a bridge with a great big troll living under it! This troll was well known for being grumpy—and for trying to eat anyone who dared to cross his bridge.

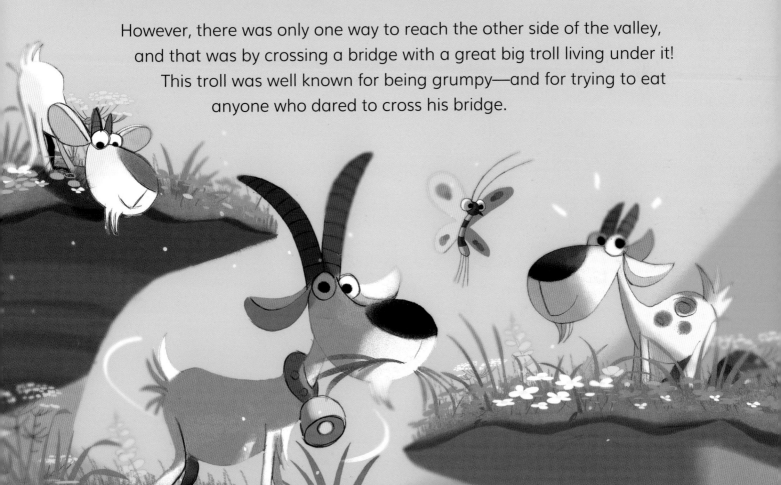

As the billy goats came closer to the bridge, brave Little Billy Goat Gruff offered to go first. Off he went—trip-trap, trip-trap—over the bridge.

When he was halfway across, the troll lurched out from his hiding place. He had a huge orange nose, wild hair, dangly ears, a crooked grin, and beady, greedy eyes. He smelled so bad that the flowers wilted on the riverbank. The little billy goat's knees knocked with fear to see him.

"Who's that trip-trapping over my bridge?" roared the troll.

"It's me, Little Billy Goat Gruff!" stammered the little goat. "Please let me pass. I'm just going to the other side of the valley so I can feast on the sweet green grass!"

"NO! I'm going to gobble you all up!" shouted the troll.

"Oh, please don't eat me," pleaded the little billy goat. "I'm so small and thin! My brother will cross the bridge soon, and he is much bigger and fatter than I am!"

The troll's eyes lit up at the thought of an even bigger meal, and he said, "Very well then, go ahead!" He let the little billy goat trip-trap his way to the other side.

It wasn't long before Medium Billy Goat Gruff decided to try his luck, too. He placed his foot nervously on the bridge, then went trip-trap, trip-trap across it, making a lot more noise than his little brother before him. Out jumped the troll again, who bellowed,

"It's me, Medium Billy Goat Gruff!" said the goat, as boldly as he could. "Please let me pass. I'm just walking to the other side of the valley so I can feast on the sweet green grass."

"NO! I'm going to gobble you all up!" boomed the troll.

"Please don't," begged the Medium Billy Goat Gruff. "My brother will be coming along soon, and he's much bigger and fatter than I am. In fact, he is the biggest of us all!"

"This must be my lucky day," grinned the troll, and he

rubbed his grumbling tummy at the thought of a big juicy goat for dinner.

"Very well then, go ahead!" he said and Medium Billy Goat Gruff trip-trapped his way to the other side of the bridge to join his little brother.

Now it was Big Billy Goat Gruff's turn to walk across the bridge, and his trip-trapping could be heard loud and clear as he walked over it.

The troll soon leaped out before him and shouted, "Who's that trip-trapping over my bridge?"

"It's me, Big Billy Goat Gruff!" said the goat, in his loudest voice. "Please let me pass. I'm just walking to the other side of the valley so I can feast on the sweet green grass."

"NO! I'm going to gobble you all up!" said the troll, licking his lips.

"Oh no, you're not," replied Big Billy Goat Gruff, "for I have two strong horns, and I'm coming to get you!"

Then Big Billy Goat Gruff lowered his horns and charged at the troll!

The troll was so surprised, he didn't move. Before he knew what was happening, Big Billy Goat Gruff had tossed him high into the air. The troll landed splashing and spluttering in the water below!

Big Billy Goat Gruff trip-trapped his way happily across the bridge to join his brothers, who were already feasting on the sweet green grass—and from that day on, the troll never again dared to bother anyone who crossed that bridge.

The Polar Bear Son

In an Inuit village on the edge of the Arctic Circle, there lived an old woman. She had no family, so the people of the village looked after her, as was their custom. The men caught fish for her, and the women shared their meals with her. Despite their kindness, the old woman was lonely and wished for a family of her own.

One day, the old woman was walking along the icy seashore when she saw a tiny polar bear cub that had strayed from its den and was lost. When no mother came, the old woman ventured up to the cub. "Poor little thing," she said, and she scooped him up in her arms. "You will be my son," she whispered, smiling at the little bear. She named him Nanuk.

She took the bear cub back to her igloo, and over the coming weeks, a strong bond grew between the old woman and her polar bear son. The children of the village all loved Nanuk, too. Every day, they came to visit the old woman, and they played with Nanuk in the snow. Her igloo echoed with their laughter.

As Nanuk and the children grew older, they taught him how to fish and hunt for seals—and Nanuk turned into the smartest and strongest hunter of all. Every day, he would go out to hunt, and then he would return home with armfuls of salmon for the old woman.

She was happy to repay the kindness of her friends and would hand them fresh fish, saying, "My Nanuk is the best fisherman in the village!"

But the men of the village soon grew jealous of Nanuk's skills. "He's making us look bad," they grumbled. "He's so good at killing seals. What if he kills a child with his clumsy paws?" And so, the men decided to get rid of Nanuk.

When the children heard what their fathers were planning, they ran to the old woman. They threw their arms around Nanuk and sobbed.

The old woman set off to visit every igloo in the village, where she

begged the men to leave her son alone. "If you harm him, you will break my heart," she cried. But the men were too proud and stubborn.

With a heavy heart, the old woman returned home. "You must leave here, Nanuk. The men don't want you here, and your life is in danger. You must go and never return."

The old woman and Nanuk clung tightly to each other. Then, with tears in his eyes, Nanuk left his igloo home. Just as she had said, the old woman's heart felt like it had broken.

For many months after Nanuk left, the old woman grieved for her son—she became thin and pale with sorrow.

The children also grieved for their lost friend, and the village became an unhappy place. The men began to feel deeply ashamed of their actions.

One day, when the old woman's heart ached with sadness, she decided to set out to find Nanuk. She left at dawn and walked all day, against chilly winds and across icy plains. As she walked, she called out Nanuk's name. Hours went by. Just as she was losing hope, she saw her polar bear son running toward her. He had grown big and strong in the time he had been gone, and his white fur shimmered in the northern light.

"Nanuk!" the old woman cried, and she wrapped her frail arms around him. Nanuk could see how tired and hungry his mother looked, so he caught some fish for her to eat and carved a snow den with his paws, so that she could keep warm. They stayed together for a day and a night, then Nanuk carried his mother home.

When the villagers saw Nanuk and thought about how far the old woman must have walked to be with him, the men bowed their heads in shame. From then on, Nanuk visited his mother every day, and the whole village welcomed him. They had learned that the love between a mother and her child should always be treated with respect.

Brer Rabbit

One sunny spring morning, Brer Fox decided to plant himself a vegetable patch. He found a lush corner of a field, and he dug, turned, and raked the soil until it looked rich and black.

When it was ready, he planted row after row of delicious peas. While Brer Fox was hard at work, Brer Rabbit had been peeking through the hedge, watching him. He dashed back to his children, and chuckling, he sang to them:

"Ti-yi! Tungalee!
I eat a pea, I pick a pea,
It grows in the ground, it grows free!
Ti-yi! Delicious peas!"

And sure enough, when Brer Fox's peas had grown and ripened, every time he went to the field to harvest his patch, he found that somebody had already been there before him, stealing the fresh pea pods from the vines. He was furious!

But Brer Fox was also no fool—he had a good idea who the culprit was. He knew it must be Brer Rabbit—but he couldn't prove it, because he always covered his tracks so well!

One afternoon, when Brer Fox had really had enough of the pea thief, he walked up and down the field, looking for a little gap in the hedge where he was sure Brer Rabbit was squeezing through. When he found the gap, he gathered some ropes and laid a trap.

The next morning, when Brer Rabbit came sneaking along, he bounded through the hedge as usual—and Brer Fox's trap sprang straight into action.

"Ti-yi! Tungalee!"

A loop of rope knotted itself around Brer Rabbit's back legs, and he was flung into the air, where he was left swinging from the top of a small tree. As he dangled there, Brer Rabbit wasn't sure whether to be scared of falling down or scared of getting stuck up there—and what he was most afraid of was what Brer Fox would do to him when he found him.

As he tried to come up with a clever excuse, he heard heavy footsteps lumbering down the road.

Soon, Brer Bear appeared, ambling along, with his paws covered in honey from a morning of bothering beehives.

Brer Rabbit called out, "Hey! Hello there, Brer Bear!"

Brer Bear was a little surprised to see Brer Rabbit dangling from a tree.

"Umm ... Hello, Brer Rabbit! How are you doing on this fine morning?"

"Thanks for asking, Brer Bear. I'm doing pretty well," said Brer Rabbit.

"What are you doing up there in the heavens, Brer Rabbit?" asked Brer Bear.

"Brer Fox is paying me a dollar a minute to guard his pea patch from the birds," said Brer Rabbit. "In fact, he said if Brer Bear comes along, you should ask him if he wants to do it instead, since he has a big family to care for and would be even better at scaring away the pesky birds."

"Wow! A dollar a minute!" thought Brer Bear. "That sounds like easy money to me!" And he jumped at Brer Rabbit's sneaky job offer.

Brer Rabbit asked his bear friend to untie the knot around his back legs and made his escape from the trap. In just a few minutes, poor Brer Bear was swinging from the top of the tree in Brer Rabbit's place.

Brer Rabbit waved goodbye to Brer Bear, then he hopped all the way over to Brer Fox's place as quickly as he could and cried out, "Brer Fox! Brer Fox! Come right away, and see the thief who's been stealing from your pea patch!"

Brer Fox dashed out of his house and ran up the lane with Brer Rabbit.

"There he is!" said Brer Rabbit, pointing at Brer Bear, who was still hanging from the tree, licking honey from his paws.

"Got you, pea thief!" cried Brer Fox, and before Brer Bear could explain how he had been tricked, Brer Fox started to holler at him, scolding him for stealing his peas.

In the middle of all this hullabaloo, Brer Rabbit slipped away to find the best hiding place he could, because he knew Brer Bear would be so angry at him for tricking him, he'd come looking for him when he was freed.

So Brer Rabbit slipped into a muddy pond and stayed there, with only his two eyes poking out. A little while later, Brer Bear came stomping down the lane in a bad mood.

"Good day, Brer Frog," he growled. "Have you seen Brer Rabbit around?"

"Yes, indeed," croaked Brer Rabbit. "He went hopping by that way a short time ago. Ribbit!"

Brer Bear ran off down the lane at great speed, and mischievous Brer Rabbit climbed out of the pond. He shook himself off, and with a grin on his face, headed for home with a secret stash of peas in his pocket.

Robin Hood and the Silver Arrow

Long ago in the forest of Sherwood, there lived a fearless outlaw by the name of Robin Hood, who was famous for stealing from the rich to give to the poor.

Robin was a hero to ordinary folk everywhere, but he was loathed by the Sheriff of Nottingham—a wicked man who ruled like a tyrant, lived like a king, and filled his coffers with the taxes he collected. The Sheriff tried again and again to capture Robin, but Robin Hood was the best archer in England—and aided by a band of merry men who fought by his side, he always escaped from the Sheriff.

Soon, the rich noblemen of the county grew scared to ride through Sherwood Forest for fear that Robin Hood would rob them. They became angry with the Sheriff for failing to imprison him. Under pressure, the Sheriff concocted a plan to put an end to his mischief and lure Robin Hood out of his forest hideout.

"I will hold an archery contest in the grounds of this castle on the last Friday of the month. The prize will be a silver arrow crafted by the finest silversmith in the county. Its feathers will be dipped in silver, and its head will be cast from solid gold. See to it that our messengers deliver this news far and wide."

The Sheriff was certain that Robin Hood wouldn't be able to resist showing off his excellent skills with a longbow, and he planned to surround the castle grounds with his soldiers, making a trap that was impossible to escape. "Robin Hood must not get away this time!" he warned.

News of the competition spread fast. When Robin Hood heard of it, he sorely wanted to win the prized silver arrow, but his merry men weren't so happy. Even Little John, Robin's most trusted friend, pleaded with him not to go.

"It's a trick, Robin—the Sheriff will ambush you the moment you step forward to shoot your arrow!"

"Then we will just have to outwit him," Robin answered courageously. "This is our chance to prove that the Sheriff can't even catch us when we walk straight into his own grounds. Let us show him what a fool he is!"

Roused by his speech, Robin Hood's band of outlaws agreed to join him.

On the day of the contest, they made their way to the Sheriff of Nottingham's castle. But rather than wearing their usual green attire to camouflage themselves among the trees, they dressed in white, red, and blue—and Robin wore a bright yellow hooded cape to conceal his face.

When they neared the castle, there were heavy crowds of spectators piling across the drawbridge, with many expert archers among them. It was the first contest of its kind, and young, old, rich, and poor were excited to see who would win the coveted prize. None of them ever imagined that Robin Hood would be foolhardy or brave enough to attempt it!

In the hustle and bustle of the crowds, it was easy for Robin and his merry men to sneak into the castle. Once inside, Robin asked the men to crowd around him until it was his turn to take a shot.

The Sheriff of Nottingham peered eagerly down from his seat on the grandstand, but as hard as he tried, he could not spot the bright green flash of Robin Hood's clothes. He was terribly frustrated that Robin hadn't turned up, but the crowd was growing impatient, so he ordered his trumpeters to signal the beginning of the archery competition. The crowd quickly fell into a hushed silence.

The first archer stepped forward and let his arrow fly, but it glanced off the edge of the target. The crowd let out a disappointed groan. Many more archers took their turns after that, but only one came close to hitting the middle—he was Guy of Gisborne, a heartless ally of the Sheriff and an old foe of Robin Hood.

Eventually, it was Robin Hood's turn. Boldly, he stepped forward and pulled down his yellow hood. The crowd gasped with surprise to see him, and the Sheriff jumped to his feet. He gave a sly smile—he had his enemy at last!

Robin lifted his longbow and prepared his arrow, then he let it fly straight into the middle of the target. A second arrow followed, splitting the first in half! There was no doubt that Robin Hood was the winner, and the crowd cheered wildly.

He bowed deeply and stepped forward to claim his prize. The Sheriff handed over the solid silver arrow and congratulated him. But just as he was about to raise his arm to signal to his guards, Robin Hood stepped back and let two more arrows fly—pinning the sleeves of the Sheriff's tunic to his chair.

The trumpeter tried to raise the alarm, but Robin spun around and shot an arrow straight into his trumpet to stop any sound from coming out! The crowd quickly cleared a path, and Robin Hood and his merry men dashed through them and leapt onto the soldiers' horses.

By the time Guy of Gisborne and the Sheriff's soldiers understood what was happening, it was too late.

Arrows flew in all directions while Robin Hood made his escape across the drawbridge. As he and his merry men galloped into the trees, Robin held his silver arrow high above his head for all to see his prize. Sherwood Forest's most famous outlaw lived to fight another day!

Jack Seeks His Fortune

There was once a young lad named Jack, who decided it was high time that he set out in the world to seek his fortune.

He hadn't gone more than a few miles before he came upon a tabby cat, curled up in the sun at the end of the lane.

"Morning, sir," mewed the cat. "Where are you heading on this fine day?"

"Why, I'm setting out to seek my fortune," said Jack, smiling proudly.

"What fun!" said the cat. "May I join you?"

"Of course," said Jack. "The more the merrier!" And off they went together— skippety-skip, skippety-skip—along the lane.

They went a little farther, and they came to a dog digging for bones.

"Morning, sir," barked the dog. "Where are you heading on this fine day?"

"I'm setting out to seek my fortune," said Jack, "along with Mistress Cat."

"May I join you?" asked the dog.

"Of course you may," said Jack. "The more the merrier!" And off they went together—yippety-yap, yippety-yap—along the lane.

The three of them went a little farther, and they came to an old billy goat chewing grass at side of the road.

"Morning, sir," bleated the goat. "Where are you heading on this fine day?"

"I'm setting out to seek my fortune," said Jack, "along with Mistress Cat and Mister Dog."

"May I join you?" asked the goat.

"Why, of course," said Jack. "The more the merrier!" And off they went together—jiggety-jog, jiggety-jog—along the lane.

The four of them went a little farther, and they came to a friendly rooster.

"Morning, sir," crowed the rooster. "Where are you heading on this fine day?"

"I'm setting out to seek my fortune," said Jack, "along with Mistress Cat, Mister Dog, and Billy Goat."

"May I join you?" said the rooster.

"Of course," said Jack. "The more the merrier!" And off they went together—stampety-stamp, stampety-stamp—along the lane.

⊙·⊙·⊙·⊙·⊙·⊙·⊙

The five fortune-seekers walked until darkness began to fall, and just as they were starting to wonder where they would spend the night, they came across an old house.

Jack told his new friends to hide in the bushes, while he crept up to the window to see if anyone was at home. Imagine Jack's surprise when he peeped inside and saw a fiendish band of burglars counting up their loot. It was a robbers' hideout!

Jack crept back to the animals and whispered, "When I give the word, let's all make as much noise as we can. On your marks, get set, go!"

So the cat mewed, the dog barked, the goat bleated, and the rooster crowed. Jack joined in and howled and yowled along with them.

Together, they made such a frightful racket that the robbers were scared for their lives. They dashed out of the house and into the woods.

⊙·⊙·⊙·⊙·⊙·⊙·⊙

Half an hour later, the robbers hadn't returned, so Jack and his adventurous animal friends went into the house and warmed themselves by the fire.

"They'll probably come back," said Jack. "We had better be prepared." So they made a plan—the cat curled up in the rocking chair, the dog hid under the table, the goat sat upstairs, the rooster flew up to the eaves, and Jack got into bed—and they waited.

In the middle of the night, when all was still, the robbers plucked up the courage to return. The leader of the band quietly tiptoed into the house to grab their loot. He wasn't gone for long before he came running out, shaking with fear.

"When I went in," he said, trembling. "I tried to sit on the rocking chair, and the ghost of an old lady moaned and stuck her knitting needles into me." That was Mistress Cat and her claws.

"Then I tried to grab the loot from the table, and the ghost of a small child howled and sank its teeth into my leg!" That was Mister Dog and his teeth.

"So I ran upstairs, and the ghost of a young boy rode into me on his tricycle and pushed me back down again." That was Billy Goat and his horns.

"But worst of all was that awful ghostly voice howling, 'Stop-the-stupid-fool!'

over and over again!" Of course, that was really clever Rooster crowing, "Cock-a-doodle-do!"

And all the time, Jack had been busily wailing like a ghost, too.

"The house must be haunted!" cried the band of robbers, quaking in their boots. Terrified, they sprinted into the woods, never to be seen again.

Jack and the four animals were given a huge reward for returning the stolen loot, and they were able to live in peace and comfort for the rest of their lives. So Jack not only made his fortune—he made four best friends!

Bambi

By Felix Salten

He came into the world in the middle of a thicket, in one of those little hidden woodland glades. There was very little room in it, barely enough for him and his mother.

He stood there, swaying unsteadily on his thin legs and staring vaguely in front of him. He hung his head, trembled a great deal, and was completely stunned.

"What a beautiful child," cried the magpie perched on a nearby branch. "What a beautiful child," she kept repeating. "How amazing to think that he should be able to get right up and walk! I've never seen anything like it. Can he run, too?"

"Of course," replied Mother softly. "But you must excuse me if I don't talk now. I have so much to do."

"Don't put yourself out because of me," said the magpie. She flew off, and the mother scarcely noticed that she was gone. She washed her newborn with her tongue, caressing his body with a warm massage.

The little thing staggered a little, then drew himself together and stood still. His little red coat, still a little tousled, had fine white spots, and on his baby face there was a sleepy expression.

Around them grew hazel bushes, dogwoods, blackthorns, and young elders. Tall maples, beeches, and oaks wove a green roof, and from the dark-brown earth sprang fern fronds.

The early sunlight filtered through the foliage, and the forest resounded with voices. The wood thrush rejoiced, doves cooed, blackbirds whistled, and finches warbled.

The little fawn understood not one of the many songs and calls. He did not even listen. Nor did he notice any of the scents that blew through the woods. He heard only the soft licking against his coat that washed and warmed him. And he smelled nothing but his mother's body.

While he suckled, his mother continued to caress her little one.

"Bambi," she whispered. Now and again, she raised her head and, listening, sniffed the air. Then she kissed her fawn again, reassured and happy. "Bambi," she repeated, "My little Bambi."

In the earliest days of Bambi's life, he walked behind his mother on a narrow track that ran through the bushes. How pleasant it was to walk there! The track appeared to be barred in a dozen places, and yet they moved forward with ease. There were tracks like this everywhere, crossing this way and that. His mother knew them all, and if Bambi stopped before a bush, she always found where the path went through.

Bambi loved to ask questions. It was the most pleasant thing for him to ask a question and to hear what answer his mother would give.

Once he asked, "Who does this trail belong to, Mother?"

His mother answered, "To us."

Bambi asked again, "To you and me?"

"Yes."

"Only to us two?"

"No," said his mother, "to us deer."

"What are deer?" Bambi asked.

His mother looked at him from head to foot and laughed. "You are a deer, and I am a deer. We're both deer," she said. "Do you understand?"

Bambi sprang into the air for joy.

"Yes, I understand," he said. "I'm a little deer and you're a big deer, aren't you?"

His mother nodded. "Now you see."

But Bambi grew serious again. "Are there other deer besides you and me?" he asked.

"Certainly," his mother said. "Many of them."

"Where are they?" cried Bambi.

"Here, everywhere."

"But I don't see them."

"You will soon," she said.

"When?" Bambi was wild with curiosity.

"Soon." The mother walked on quietly. Bambi followed her, wondering what "soon" might mean.

They walked along. Presently, it grew light ahead of them. The trail ended with a tangle of vines and bushes. A few steps more, and they were in a bright, open space that spread out before them. Bambi wanted to bound forward, but his mother had stopped.

"What is it?" he asked impatiently.

"It's the meadow," his mother answered.

"What is a meadow?" asked Bambi insistently.

"You'll soon find out," she said. She had become serious and watchful.

She stood motionless, holding her head high and listening intently.

"It's all right now," she said, "we can go out."

Bambi leaped forward, but his mother barred the way.

"Wait till I call you," she said. Bambi obeyed at once and stood still. "That's right," said his mother. "Now listen to what I say."

"Walking in the meadow isn't simple," his mother went on. "It's a difficult and dangerous business. Now do exactly as I tell you to. Will you?"

"Yes," Bambi promised.

"Good," said his mother. "I'm going out alone first. Wait here. And don't take your eyes off me. If you see me run back, then turn and run as fast as you can. I'll catch up with you soon."

She went on earnestly. "Run away as fast as your legs will carry you. Run even if something should happen, even if you see me fall to the ground. Don't think of me, do you understand? No matter what you see or hear, run as fast as you possibly can. Do you promise to do that?"

"Yes," said Bambi softly. His mother spoke so seriously.

"Now I'm going ahead," said his mother. She walked out.

Bambi saw how she moved with slow, cautious steps. He stood there full of fear and curiosity. He saw how his mother listened in all directions, then grew calm again. She looked around, satisfied, and called, "Come!"

Bambi bounded out. Joy seized him with such tremendous force that he forgot his worries in a flash. Through the thicket, he could catch a glimpse of the blue sky, but now the heavens stretched far and wide. The sunlight was beaming down, and he stood in the splendid warmth with his eyes closed. He stretched his young limbs joyfully. He drank in the air. The sweet smell of the meadow made him happy.

If he had been a child, he would have shouted. But he was a young deer, so he leaped into the air three, four times.

He was overcome with the desire to leap and jump. His mother was glad. She bent laughingly toward Bambi for a moment. Then she was off with one bound, racing around so that the tall grass stems swished.

Bambi was frightened and stood still. She came up with a wonderful swishing sound and stopped two steps from him. Laughing, she cried, "Catch me." And in a flash, she was gone.

Bambi started after her. He took a few steps. Then his steps became short bounds. He felt as if he were flying without any effort on his part. Bambi was beside himself with joy.

The swishing grass sounded wonderful to his ears. It was amazingly soft and as fine as silk where it brushed against him. He ran around in a circle. He flew off in a new circle, turned around again, and kept running.

Suddenly, the race was over. He came up to his mother, lifting his hoofs elegantly. He looked joyfully at her.

Then they strolled along, side by side. Bambi began to look around the meadow, and its wonders amazed him. Blade after blade of grass covered every inch of the ground. It bent softly aside under every footstep. The green meadow was starred with daisies, red and purple clover blossoms, and bright, golden dandelions.

"Look, look, Mother!" Bambi exclaimed. "There's a flower flying."

"That's not a flower," said his mother, "that's a butterfly."

Bambi stared at the butterfly. It had darted lightly from a blade of grass and was fluttering about its giddy way. Then Bambi saw there were many butterflies in the air. He longed to see one close up.

"Look! See that piece of grass jumping," cried Bambi.

"Look how high it jumps!"

"That's not grass!" his mother said. "That's a nice grasshopper."

"Why does he jump?" asked Bambi.

"Because we're walking here," his mother answered. "He's afraid we'll step on him."

"Oh," said Bambi, turning to the grasshopper, who was sitting on a daisy. "You don't have to be afraid. We won't hurt you."

"I'm not afraid," the grasshopper replied in a quavering voice. "I was only frightened for a moment."

"Excuse us for disturbing you," said Bambi shyly.

"Not at all," the grasshopper quavered. "Since it's you, it's perfectly all right. I haven't time to gossip, though, I have to look for my wife. Hop!" And he vanished.

Talking to the grasshopper had excited Bambi, as it was the first time he had ever

spoken to a stranger. He noticed a flower moving in the grasses. No, it was a butterfly. Bambi crept closer.

The butterfly hung heavily on a grass stem and fanned its wings slowly.

"Please sit still," Bambi said.

"Why would I sit still? I'm a butterfly!" the insect answered in astonishment.

"Oh, please," Bambi pleaded. "I want so much to look at you. Please?"

"Very well," said the butterfly, "but not for long."

Bambi stood in front of him. "How truly beautiful you are!" he cried. "How wonderfully beautiful, like a flower!"

"What?" cried the butterfly, fanning his wings. "In my circle, it's thought that we're handsomer than flowers."

Bambi was embarrassed. "Oh, yes, much handsomer, excuse me." Bambi was enchanted.

"Oh, you are handsomer than flowers," cried Bambi. "Besides, you can fly and flowers can't, that's why."

The butterfly spread his wings and fluttered into the sunny air. He soared so lightly that Bambi could hardly follow him, then he balanced in the air and said, "Now I must fly away."

And that was Bambi's first time in the meadow.

Lazy Jack

There was once a boy named Jack, who lived at home with his mother. She worked hard at the spinning wheel all day to earn enough to feed them both, but Jack did nothing.

In summer, he would spend all day lazing in the sunshine; and come winter, he would put his feet up by the fire, while his poor mother spun at the wheel with icy-cold fingers. No matter how much she begged him, Jack wouldn't get a job.

After a while, his mother grew so frustrated, she told Jack that if he didn't earn his keep, she would have to throw him out!

of milk. Remembering his mother's advice, he tucked the pitcher under his arm. But by the time he got home, most of the milk had spilled.

"Oh, Jack!" cried his mother. "You should have carried it on your head!"

"Ah, yes!" said Jack. "Don't worry. I'll do that next time."

The following day, Jack found work with the cheesemaker, who paid him with a big wheel of cheese. Recalling his mother's wise words, Jack carried the cheese on his head. But the sun was beating down, and by the time he got home, the cheese had melted in his hair and was completely runny!

Jack knew that she was completely serious. Early the next morning, he visited the local grocer, who offered him a penny for a day's work.

However, as Jack was walking home that night, he jumped over a stream and dropped his penny in it. It was swept away before he could grab it.

"Oh, you silly boy!" said his mother. "Why didn't you put it in your pocket?"

"I'll be sure to do that next time!" promised Jack.

So the next day, Jack looked for work again. This time, he did a day's work at the dairy in return for a little pitcher

"Jack tried to carry the kitten home"

"Oh, Jack!" his mother moaned. "You should have carried it in your hands!"

"Yes, Mother," said Jack. "I'll make sure I remember that next time."

Jack went out again the next day, but the only work he could find was with the baker, who paid him with a kitten. Jack tried to carry the kitten home in his hands, as his mother had told him, but the kitten scratched and clawed at Jack's arms and face so much that he had to let it go. That night, he went home empty-handed.

"Oh, Jack," sighed his mother. "You should have tied a string around its neck and led it behind you!"

"Of course! You're right, Mother," said Jack. "I'll try that next time."

The next morning, Jack set off again to find work. This time, he got a job with the butcher, who paid him with a shoulder of lamb. As his mother had suggested, he tied some string around the meat and trailed it behind him, dragging it through the dirt all the way. By the time he got home, the meat was ruined.

"What on earth is the matter with you, boy?" wailed his mother, who had run out of patience with him by now. "Why didn't you carry it on your shoulder?"

"Oh, that's a good idea, Mother!" said Jack. "Don't worry, I promise I'll do that next time."

The next day, Jack found some work with the local miller, who paid him with a donkey. Determined not to let his mother down and get kicked out of her house, Jack used all his strength to heave the donkey up onto his shoulders, and he started to stagger home, his knees knocking all the way.

Now it so happened that, along the way, Jack passed the house of a rich man who had a daughter who had never spoken or smiled. The best doctors in the country had tried to help the girl, but each one had declared that there was no cure for her condition.

However, when she looked out of her window and saw Jack lurching along the dusty road with a donkey on his shoulders, its feet waving in the air, she burst into fits of laughter and shouted out, "Have you ever seen such a funny sight?" The girl ran outside to talk to Jack, followed by her astounded parents.

Jack and the girl laughed together so much that day, that her father offered Jack a job entertaining his daughter, and Jack's mother was finally able to retire. From that day on, Lazy Jack got a new name—he became known as Jack.

The Tortoise and the Geese

There was once a tortoise who loved nothing more than to talk and tell stories—especially stories about himself.

Next to the great lake where he lived, he entertained everyone with his tall tales and imaginative adventures, in which he was always the brave hero. From sunrise to sunset, he chattered so much, there was barely time for any of the other animals to speak.

One day, two geese stopped at the lake to rest, and they listened to the tortoise telling his stories. He was delighted to have a new audience, and when he finished, he asked them where they had come from.

The geese told him that they had migrated many hundreds of miles over mountains and seas to escape from winter storms. They were on their way to a lake of turquoise-blue water, where the days were always long and warm.

Their description sparked a deep longing in the tortoise's heart, and for once, he was silent.

"It's all very well telling tales of my adventures," thought the tortoise, sadly, "but I've never been anywhere other than back and forth between my burrow and this lake."

Suddenly, he felt overwhelmed with the need to soar over mountains and seas. "What stories I'll be able to tell!" he thought. "How my audience will admire me! Why, I'll be famous!"

"When you leave, can you take me with you?" begged the tortoise.

The geese looked at him in surprise. "But you're too heavy to carry, and we need all our wings to fly!"

The tortoise thought for a moment. "What if we use a stick?" he suggested. "You can hold it between your beaks, and I can hang on to it with my mouth."

The other animals sniggered, and the snake hissed with laughter. "You do know that this means you will have to keep your mouth shut, don't you?" snapped the crocodile.

"I promise to be completely silent!" announced the tortoise. "Starting as soon as we set out tomorrow."

The geese agreed to the plan, and the tortoise continued telling his tales until the sun sank behind the mountain.

The following day, the geese prepared for the next part of their journey, while the tortoise found a strong stick.

"Are you really sure about this?" asked the geese.

"Definitely!" said the tortoise.

"And you promise not to talk?"

"Absolutely!" promised the tortoise.

"You do know that if you open your mouth, you will be dropped from a great height and fall to the ground?"

"Indeed!" nodded the tortoise. "I vow to say nothing between now and the moment we land."

Then he gripped the stick tightly, and the geese took off, at first lumbering across the lake and eventually soaring high into the sky. The tortoise was astonished by the view and found it very difficult not to comment on it.

Soon, the geese passed over a city. When the people looked up and saw them struggling along with a stick between their beaks and something large dangling from it, they were most confused.

"What is that great lump those geese are carrying?" they cried.

"Great lump?" thought the tortoise. "How dare they call me such a thing!" So he shouted down to them, "Hey, I'm no great lump! I'm the tortoise adventurer, and I'm going to be famous far and wide!"

And because he had opened his mouth, he lost his grip on the stick and went tumbling to the ground, where he smashed his shell in half.

The tortoise did become famous far and wide, but for all the wrong reasons—he became famous for not listening to good advice and for not being able to keep his mouth shut!

Cat and Mouse

You might not believe it, but there was once a tabby cat that decided to make friends with the little mouse that lived just around the corner.

Naturally, at first the little mouse was very timid —she had spent most of her life running away from cats. But the tabby cat was so pleasant and spoke so kindly of how clever and brave the little mouse was, that she was soon thoroughly charmed.

After a few weeks of meeting for tea and a chat, the cat invited the mouse to come and live with her. "We'll have such fun together!" the cat said, smiling, and the mouse agreed.

"But winter is not far away," said the cat. "We should gather some supplies, so that we don't starve."

On the morning the mouse was moving into the cat's home, she spotted a jar of thick cream on someone's doorstep. "That will be perfect for winter!" she thought, and the smart little mouse tipped the jar over and rolled it all the way to the cat's house.

The cat was delighted. "We must hide it where nobody can find it. This will keep us going all winter." They both thought long and hard. "I've got just the place!" said the mouse. "Let's hide it under the altar in the church at the end of the street. Nobody ever looks there!"

And so the pair rolled the heavy jar down the street, all the way up the aisle of the church, and then tucked it away under the altar.

They promised each other that they wouldn't touch it until they absolutely needed it.

A few weeks went by, and the cat found that she couldn't stop thinking about the cream. She longed for it so badly that, one morning, she said to the mouse, "I forgot to mention, my cousin has had a kitten, and they invited me to the christening at the church today. Do you mind if I go?"

"Of course not!" said the mouse. "You go and enjoy yourself. And if you see anything good to eat, bring me back a crumb or two!"

The cat said goodbye, then stalked up the street to the church, crept up the aisle, and sneaked under the altar. She peeled back the lid of the jar and licked the thickest, creamiest part off the top. It was even more delicious than she had imagined! She spent the rest of the day lazing in a sunny spot on the church roof, licking her long whiskers.

When she returned in the evening, the mouse said, "You look like you've had fun! Was it a good day?"

"Indeed it was," grinned the cat.

"What did they call their kitten?"

The cat hesitated for a second then said, "Oh, it was ... Top-Off."

"Top-Off?" laughed the mouse. "What an unusual name!"

A few weeks passed, and the cat found herself thinking about the jar of cream again, so she said to the mouse, "I've just heard that another of my cousins has had a kitten, and it's being christened today. Would you mind if I went?"

"Not at all!" said the mouse. "You enjoy yourself; I'll tidy up here."

"Oh, I will!" smiled the cunning cat, and she set off for the church again.

Hiding under the altar, she peeled the top off the cream once more and devoured half the jar. "Scrumptious," purred the cat, and she curled up in a warm spot and fell asleep.

She went home with a full belly later that day, and the little mouse asked, "Did it go well?"

"Oh, very well," replied the cat.

"And what did they call the kitten?"

"Hmm ... Half-Empty," said the cat.

"Half-Empty!" exclaimed the mouse. "I've never heard of such a strange name!" But the good-natured mouse didn't think too much of it.

Life was normal for a few weeks, and the cat and mouse lived together in harmony. But it was starting to get chilly, and the cat's thoughts turned again to the jar of cream.

"It tastes so much better because I don't have to share it," she thought, and her mouth began to water.

"Little friend," said the cat, "can you believe that another of my cousins has had a kitten? The christening takes place today, and I'd love to go. I hear that this kitten is very rare—it is completely black with white paws."

"How nice!" said the mouse. "Have a good time—I'll see you later. The house will be tidy when you return."

The greedy cat slinked away to the church where, once again, she hid beneath the altar and polished off what was left of their precious jar of cream. It took some time to lick her whiskers clean.

Feeling fat and full, she walked back to the house. The mouse greeted her warmly. "Did you have a fine time?"

"Oh yes," yawned the cat. "It was a very fine day."

"And what did they call their special kitten? Paws? Mittens? Boots?"

The cat sighed and thought for a moment, then replied, "All-Gone."

"All-Gone?" puzzled the little mouse. "Such an odd name for a sweet little kitten!" But the mouse trusted her friend, so she said no more.

A whole month went by without any christenings, but the nights were drawing in, the days were

colder, and it was getting harder to hunt for food. Every teeny morsel found by the cat and mouse was shared between the two of them.

One chilly night, the mouse's tummy was rumbling so much, she cried, "Dear cat, I think it's time we paid a visit to our special jar of cream—we are both hungry, and we have waited long enough."

The mouse scurried off to the church, with the cat following close behind. When she reached the altar and found the empty cream jar, the mouse knew that she had been a fool.

"Of course," she sighed, sadly.

"All those visits to the church ... Top-Off, Half-Empty, and All-Gone. How silly I have been to trust you!"

"Yes," agreed the cat, "and now I've had quite enough of sharing my food with you, so I'm going to eat you, too!"

The cat had scarcely finished talking when she pounced on the mouse and tried to catch her. However, the mouse was not about to be fooled again. In a flash, she darted down the aisle, and in the blink of a cat's eye, she made her escape through the church door. Needless to say, she never made friends with a cat again!

The Three Sillies

Once there was a farmer and his wife, and they had one daughter. Soon after the daughter's eighteenth birthday, she met a fine country gentleman, and she liked him very much.

He came to visit her every day, and the daughter and her parents were certain he would soon ask for her hand in marriage. Excited at the idea of such a good match, they invited him to supper to impress him.

The farmer and his wife served the gentleman a hearty meal, and the daughter went down to the cellar to fetch some more beer. But as she was pouring, she looked up and spied a mallet hanging from the beam above the beer keg.

Her mind started to wander, and she thought to herself, "What if we were to get married and have a son, and what if my son came down here to pour beer from the keg, and the mallet fell on his head and hurt him?

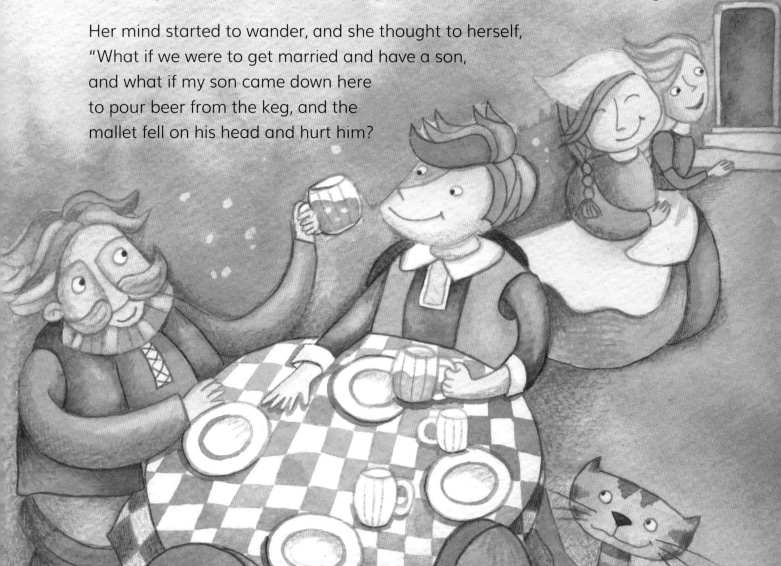

Oh, wouldn't it be dreadful?" And with that, she started to cry.

After a while, the farmer and his wife wondered why their daughter was taking so long, so the wife went down to the cellar to check on her. She found her daughter in a pool of tears and beer pouring all over the floor.

"What is the matter?" cried the wife.

"Oh, Mother!" sobbed the girl. "Do you see that mallet there? Imagine if I were to get married and have a son, and he came down here to pour beer from the keg, and the mallet fell on his head and hurt him! Wouldn't it be dreadful?"

"Goodness me!" said the mother. "That would be dreadful!" And she sat down beside her daughter and burst into tears.

By now, the farmer was getting worried, so he went down to the cellar and found both his daughter and his wife in floods of tears, and beer pouring all over the floor.

"What is the matter?" he cried.

"Oh, husband!" wept his wife. "Do you see that mallet there? Imagine if our dear daughter here were to get married and have a son, and he came down here

to pour beer from the keg, and the mallet fell on his head and hurt him! Wouldn't that be dreadful?"

"Dear, oh dear!" said the farmer. "That would be dreadful indeed!" And he sat beside his daughter and wife, and he started crying, too.

Now, all this time, the gentleman had been wondering where his hosts were. Eventually, he went down to the cellar to see what was happening.

He was surprised to find the farmer, his wife, and their daughter all crying, and beer pouring all over the floor.

"What on earth are you all doing, sitting there sobbing and letting beer pour all over the floor?" he cried.

"Do you see that mallet there?" wept the farmer. "Imagine if our daughter were to marry you and have a son, and he came down here to pour beer from the keg, and the mallet fell on his head and hurt him! Oh, wouldn't it be dreadful?"

The gentleman burst into laughter, reached up, grabbed the mallet, and placed it on the floor.

"I have visited many places and met many people, and I can honestly say that I have never met anyone more silly than the three of you! I'll tell you what—I'm setting off on more travels next week. If I can find three bigger sillies than you, then I promise that I will return and ask for your daughter's hand in marriage."

He wished them goodbye, and all three of them burst into tears again at how very silly they had been.

The following week, the gentleman set out on his travels. He hadn't gone far when he came across a woman who was trying to persuade a very reluctant cow to climb up a ladder onto the roof of her cottage.

"May I ask what you are doing, madam?" asked the gentleman.

"Look at that grass on my roof!" she exclaimed. "I'm trying to get the cow up there to eat it. I've tied a string

around her neck, and I'll drop the other end down the chimney to tie around my waist. Then she'll be safe!"

The gentleman was puzzled. "Why can't you just cut the grass and throw it down for the cow?" he asked, but the woman would hear nothing of it.

She heaved the cow up the ladder, then dropped the string down the chimney, and she dashed inside to tie the other end around her waist.

Moments later, the cow fell off the roof of the cottage, and the woman shot up the chimney and got stuck up there. Her friends came rushing to help.

"Now that was one big silly!" thought the gentleman and went on his way.

Night was falling, so the gentleman looked for a place to sleep. The local inn was busy, so he agreed to share a room with a stranger, who seemed like a friendly fellow. However, the next morning, the gentleman was surprised to see the fellow hang his trousers from the handles of a chest of drawers, run across the room, and try to jump into them!

The strange fellow tried to jump into his trousers several times, but always ended up on the floor.

"May I ask what you are doing, sir?" asked the gentleman.

"Aren't trousers annoying?" said the fellow. "Who invented such a silly item of clothing? It takes me over an hour to jump into mine every morning!"

The gentleman started laughing, then took his own trousers and showed him how to put them on. The fellow was grateful and said that he would never have thought of doing it that way!

The gentleman left the room, chuckling to himself. "That was another big silly!" he said.

He continued on his journey, walking all day long, until night fell again. He eventually reached a small village, and in the middle of the village, there was a crowd of people gathered around a pond, holding rakes, nets, and brooms. They all seemed to be reaching for something in the pond and grumbling loudly.

"May I ask what you are doing?" asked the gentleman.

"It's a terrible thing!" said one of the villagers, holding a fishing net over the water.
"The moon has tumbled into our village pond, and we can't seem to get it out!"

The gentleman explained kindly that the moon was still in the sky, and they were just seeing its reflection in the pond, but the villagers thought he was trying to make a fool of them. They chased him away, waving their fists at him.

The gentleman galloped away, laughing to himself. "Now, they were definitely the biggest sillies of them all!" he thought. So that was three sillies, all in all!

There and then, the gentleman decided to set off for home. When he got there, he went straight to the farmer's daughter and asked if she would marry him. She agreed, and the two went on to have many silly times together.

The Selkie Wife

Long ago, on the Orkney Islands off the coast of Scotland, there lived a fisherman who spent most of his time at sea.

One blustery day, after battling the wild waves and with only a small catch to show for it, the fisherman headed home to his cottage on the beach. As he moored his boat, he heard beautiful voices singing a melodic tune—it sent tingles down his spine to hear it. Across the bay, he saw a group of people splashing around in the sea, laughing and singing.

"I must be dreaming!" mumbled the fisherman. "Who in their right mind would play in these icy waters at this time in the evening?" He walked toward them. As he drew close, the swimmers caught sight of him. They stopped what they were doing and suddenly dived into the water and disappeared!

However, there on the shore lay a velvety sealskin. The fisherman was amazed. "The legends are true! Those people were Selkies!"

The Orkney Isles are famous for their legendary tales about Selkies—seals who can remove their skins and take on human form—but very few people have actually seen them, so he couldn't believe his luck. "Imagine how much money I can sell this skin for—and when people hear what I saw, it will be worth even more!"

The fisherman felt very pleased with himself. However, as he reached his cottage, he heard sobbing. The most beautiful woman he had ever seen, with hair down to her waist, was sitting on the beach weeping with sorrow. It was heartbreaking to hear.

"Sweet lady, why do you cry?" asked the fisherman.

"I'm crying because you have my sealskin," wept the lady. "I am one of the Selkie folk, and without it, I can't swim home."

Though the fishermen knew that he should return the skin to the lady, he longed to get to know her better, so he clutched it more tightly.

"Must you go home?" he asked. "Perhaps we can talk?"

"But I belong to the sea!" said the lady. "And the Selkie folk will be so worried about me!"

But the fisherman had fallen very suddenly and stubbornly in love with her.

Giving the lady his most charming smile and still gripping the sealskin, he pleaded, "Why not spend three days with me? I will take care of you. I'll catch fresh fish for you. You might not find living on land so bad."

"It seems I have no choice," said the lady, with great sadness. "I can't go home without my skin." And so she went with him to his cottage, where he hid the sealskin in a secret nook up the chimney. For three days, he treated her like a princess.

At the end of that time, instead of returning the sealskin, he begged, "Just one more day, sweet lady." This went on for many days, and soon, the days turned into weeks and months.

Eventually, it seemed as though the lady hadn't remembered her life under the sea, and she agreed to marry the fisherman. He loved his Selkie wife with all his heart and treated her with kindness. And whenever he caught her looking longingly at the sea, he would do his best to cheer her up.

Over the years, the fisherman and his Selkie wife had seven children—four boys and three girls—who they loved very dearly. They were a happy family, and the children loved to play in the sea, but their mother would never join in, no matter how much they begged.

"Mother, please come swimming with us!" they pleaded, and she would just shake her head and give a sad smile.

One day, when the husband was out fishing with his three eldest sons and the daughters were on the beach, the youngest of the boys found his mother staring at the sea and crying.

"Why do you always look so sad when you look at the sea?" asked the boy.

"Because I was born there, son," said his mother, without thinking. "And I can't go back because your father has hidden my sealskin."

"You're a Selkie!" gasped her son. "I know where your skin is!" And he reached up the chimney breast and dragged down the hidden sealskin.

"I found it one day when I was playing, but I didn't know what it was!"

The Selkie wife held the sealskin in her hands, then hugged her son tightly and kissed him on the forehead.

"Thank you, sweet child. I will always love you and your brothers and sisters, and I will come back as often as I can, but I must return to where I belong. I've waited so many years for this day."

Then she ran down to the shoreline and slipped on her sealskin for the first time in many years.

The little boy followed her and smiled as he saw his mother happily dive into the waves—her true home. She turned and waved goodbye to him and her three daughters, then she disappeared under the surf, where she changed back into a seal again.

On her journey back to the Selkie folk and her secret home in the sea, the wife passed the fisherman's boat and stopped to watch him and her three sons rowing back to the beach.

When the fisherman saw the seal splashing in the waves, he thought he saw something familiar in its eyes, and when he reached the shore, his young son told him what had happened. The fisherman's heart ached to hear the news, but he understood how brave and kind his child had been—and how wrong he had been to keep his wife away from her home for all those years.

From that day on, whenever the Selkie wife came to visit her family—which she often did—there was great joy and lots of singing. She often played with her children in the sea, letting them ride on her back or dive beneath the surface for rare shells. It was just as it should have been, and everyone was very happy, even the fisherman.

Town Mouse and Country Mouse

Once there were two mice who were cousins—one lived in a large house in a big town, and the other lived in a tiny cottage in the countryside. They hadn't seen each other for a long time, so Country Mouse invited Town Mouse to come and stay with her.

When Town Mouse arrived, Country Mouse was very excited—she had worked hard to make things as nice as possible for her cousin. She said, "You must be hungry after your long journey. I have been out in the fields this morning, and I have gathered us a fine feast!"

Town Mouse sat on a small wooden stool, while Country Mouse emptied out her secret store and laid the table with nuts, berries, and a hearty bean soup.

"Oh!" exclaimed Town Mouse, "Is this what you eat in the countryside? I'm really not used to plain food like this. In town, we dine on fancy dishes, such as pastries and cakes and other delights."

Town Mouse's words made Country Mouse feel sad, but Town Mouse didn't notice. She looked around Country Mouse's small cottage, which was just one room with a bed in the corner. "In my house, there are many rooms and stairs that lead up to even more rooms!" she said.

"There is a grand dining room and a large kitchen with cupboards that are bursting with food. We can eat and drink whenever we like, and we never have to go out in the fields to gather it. Town life is so much easier than country life," she sighed.

Country Mouse showed Town Mouse the lovely fields of flowers around her cottage and took her to the pretty babbling brook, but all weekend, Town Mouse talked about how her life was so much more exciting in the town.

At the end of the weekend, Town Mouse said, "I don't understand how you put up with living here! Come and stay with me for a few days, and I will show you the fine life. You'll soon wonder how you ever lived in the countryside!"

Country Mouse felt so downhearted about her home that she took Town Mouse up on her offer. She packed a small suitcase and set off with her cousin to the town.

When they arrived, the buildings were so close together and so tall that Country Mouse felt that she could barely see the sky—and it was so noisy, she covered her poor ears. But when Town Mouse showed Country Mouse her house, she thought it a very splendid sight indeed.

"Let's eat after our long journey!" said Town Mouse, and she led Country Mouse to the dining room. Here, Country Mouse was amazed! There on the table were the leftovers of a huge feast. There were cakes, tarts, pies, and piles of glistening fruit. There was fresh bread, slices of cheese, and all manner of treats!

When they had eaten, Town Mouse led the way to the kitchen for something to drink, but just as Country Mouse sipped some cool water, she heard a loud and terrifying sound behind her. She turned just in time to see a giant paw with sharp claws swipe at her. Country Mouse was terrified and dashed away as quickly as she could, but the cat was close behind her.

Country Mouse quickly leaped into a small hole and found Town Mouse hiding there, too. "Who is that?" asked Country Mouse, trembling with fright.

"Oh, that's just one of the cats we share the house with," said Town Mouse. "It's all right, as long as you can run very quickly and dodge their sharp claws!"

At that, Country Mouse grabbed her suitcase and scurried to the front door.

"Goodbye, cousin!" said Country Mouse. "I would rather live a simple country life in peace than a life of feasts and fear!"

And Country Mouse set off home for her little cottage in the countryside.

The Blind Friends and the Elephant

There were once six blind friends who lived in a village in India. They had just sat down for lunch one day, when they heard the village children cry with excitement, "An elephant! An elephant! There's an elephant by the watering hole!"

The six friends decided to visit the watering hole and get to know what an elephant looks like by touching it with their hands. "It might be useful for us to know," said one of the friends, wisely.

They set off for the watering hole, but as they drew closer to the elephant, one of the friends tripped and fell against the side of its body.

"Wow," he said, feeling the elephant's side with his hands. "I can tell you that this elephant looks exactly like a brick wall—and it's as big as a wall, too!"

"You're wrong!" said his friend, who by now was twirling the elephant's tail. "This elephant has a body as thin as a rope! There's nothing to him."

"Not at all," piped up another of the friends, who was stroking the elephant's trunk. "It is much smoother than a rope —this elephant is just like a snake." And she quickly let go of the trunk.

"What on earth are you talking about?" puzzled the fourth friend, who was gripping the elephant's tusk. "This is no snake—it's long and sharp and pointed. This elephant is carrying a spear—and here's a second one!"

"Don't be silly," said the fifth friend,

"There's nothing to fear here—all I can feel is a sturdy tree trunk. This elephant won't do us any harm!"

And finally, the sixth friend cried, "None of you are right. I've found a fan here, and it's keeping me lovely and cool!" She was standing under one of the elephant's large ears.

"Nonsense!" said the first friend, and they all broke into a noisy argument about what the elephant looked like.

Soon, the children, who were playing by the watering hole, came to see what the commotion was all about.

"Why are you arguing?" they asked.

"We can't agree on what this elephant looks like," said one of the friends, and they each started to explain what they had seen with their hands.

"Well," said the children, "you are all right! You each touched a different part of the elephant, so you all saw something different. Just put it all together, and you have an elephant!"

The blind friends felt silly—if only they had listened to each other instead of arguing, they would have known what an elephant looked like much sooner!

The Wish Fish

There was once a fisherman and his wife, and they lived in a shabby little shack by the sea.

One day, the fisherman was out at sea when he caught an extraordinary flounder. Its scales looked like pure gold, and when the fisherman hauled it onto the boat, it pleaded, "Sir, I beg you to let me live. Put me back in the water, and I'll show you just how special I am."

"You already have!" cried the fisherman. "I've never met a talking fish before!" And he quickly released the golden flounder into the sea. It disappeared under the waves for a second, then bobbed up to the top again and said, "To show you my thanks, I will grant you a wish. What would you like?"

"Well," said the fisherman, "I am a happy soul, but I know that my wife would like a nice cottage with a pretty little garden, please."

"Go home," said the flounder. "Your wish is granted."

The fisherman dashed home, where he found a sweet little cottage with a living room, a bedroom, and a kitchen. Outside, there was a pretty garden with flowers and a vegetable patch, just as he had hoped. He explained to his wife what had happened.

"Now we can live well," he smiled, but his wife just nodded and said, "Hmm ... Let's see."

After a week, she began to complain. "Husband, this cottage is too small.

I can't help thinking that you made a mistake. You should have asked for something bigger. Can you ask the fish for a mansion instead?"

"But he only just gave us this cottage!" said the fisherman.

"Just ask!" insisted the wife. "I'm sure he won't mind."

The fisherman liked their new cottage, but he sailed out to sea and called:

"Golden flounder in the sea,
Can you grant a wish for me?"

After a while, the flounder popped its head above the waves. "What do you want, fisherman?" it asked.

"I love our cottage, but my wife has asked for a large mansion."

"Go home," said the flounder. "Your wish is granted."

⋈⋈⋈⋈⋈⋈⋈⋈⋈

The fisherman sailed for home again and there, before him, stood a grand mansion. A servant opened the door, revealing a huge hallway, a carved wooden staircase, and many large rooms. His wife was telling her other servants what to do.

"Now we can be happy!" smiled the fisherman. But his wife just shrugged and said, "Maybe."

All was well for a few weeks, but one morning, the wife said, "What fools we have been, husband! We should have asked for a castle. You must sail to the fish and ask for a castle instead!"

"But we have everything we need here," said the fisherman.

"I don't," said the wife. "I want more!"

And so, with a heavy heart, the fisherman went out to sea and called:

"Golden flounder in the sea,
Can you grant a wish for me?"

The flounder soon appeared and said, "What is it now, fisherman?"

"It's my wife," sighed the fisherman. "She thinks we should have a castle."

"Go home," said the flounder. "Your wish is granted."

The fisherman returned home to find his wife standing outside a magnificent stone castle.

Inside, there was a huge staircase and a banqueting hall with golden chairs and tables, and many more rooms. In the grounds, there were stables, gardens, and a wonderful fountain.

"What a beautiful castle," gasped the fisherman. "Now we can be satisfied." But his wife just said, "Perhaps."

Early the next morning, she shook the fisherman awake. "I've been thinking. What is the point of owning a castle if I'm not a queen? You must ask the flounder to grant this wish for me, or we'll never be happy!"

"But I am happy!" said the fisherman.

"I'm not," answered his wife. "Get up. You must go immediately."

The fisherman got dressed, and off he sailed to see the flounder.

"Golden flounder in the sea,
Can you grant a wish for me?"

The fish sighed to see the fisherman there again. "Well?" it said.

"My wife thinks that she should be a queen now," mumbled the fisherman.

"Go home," said the flounder. "Your wish is granted."

When the fisherman arrived home, he was greeted by a trumpet fanfare, and a royal courtier placed a crown on his head. "Her Royal Highness is in the throne room, sire," said the courtier.

The fisherman felt silly in his fishing clothes and crown. When he found his wife, she was perched on a throne, which was decorated with diamonds.

"You are queen," said the fisherman. "At last, you can be happy."

"No!" said his wife. "I'm not happy. I don't like how the sun shines in my eyes or how the breeze blows under the doors. I have decided I need to rule the world, so that I can change these things. Can you ask the fish?"

"I can't ask for that! The flounder has already given us so much."

But his wife moaned and moaned, so the fisherman set off over the waves and called out wearily:

"Golden flounder in the sea,
Can you grant a wish for me?"

The flounder took a while to appear. "You again!" groaned the fish.

Feeling embarrassed, the fisherman said, "My wife wants to rule the world."

"What?" said the flounder. "Fine. Go home, and you will see that she now has everything she deserves."

The fisherman made his way home, and when he got there, he laughed out loud to see his wife sitting on a little wooden stool outside the shack they first lived in.

Happy to have his old life back, he never again called for the flounder— and his wife finally had to learn how to be satisfied with what she had.

Mouse Deer and the Tiger

One day, Mouse Deer was taking a sip of cool water from the stream, when a hungry tiger came stalking up behind her, licking his lips in anticipation of a fine lunch.

Mouse Deer saw the tiger's reflection and knew that she wouldn't be able to run away because the tiger was much too fast. She had to think quickly. As the tiger hunched down, ready to leap on her, she turned around and said, "Hey, tiger! I know you're probably hungry right now, but if you eat me, you'll get in a whole lot of trouble with the king!"

"Ha! Why would the king care about a pathetic little creature like you?" sneered the tiger, looking disbelieving.

"Oh, I'm not just any creature! I guard the king's most prized cake—a cake so special and delicious that only the royal family is allowed to eat it!"

Mouse Deer pointed at a shiny black dome at the edge of the lake. It didn't look much like a cake, and it certainly didn't look very appealing, but the tiger was curious.

"I was once allowed to nibble on it, and I can tell you that it tastes a lot better than it looks," Mouse Deer assured him.

"In fact, it is the best cake ever made. And I heard from the royal court that just one of these cakes will satisfy your hunger for a whole month!"

"Can I try it?" asked the tiger.

"Certainly not!" gasped Mouse Deer. "The king would have me executed if I allowed anyone to eat his cake!"

"Well, you have a choice," growled the tiger. "I'm hungry, so either I eat the king's cake, or I eat you!"

dung! The tiger's face creased with disgust, and he spat out the mouthful. Mouse Deer had fooled him!

"Mouse Deer!" he roared. "Just wait till I find you!" And he, too, went bounding into the trees, determined to catch Mouse Deer and punish her.

It was several days before the tiger bumped into Mouse Deer in a forest clearing, and he was still furious.

"There you are!" snarled the tiger. "How dare you trick someone as powerful and important as I am? You won't get away so easily this time!"

Mouse Deer wondered how she was going to get out of this one. The tiger was preparing to pounce when Mouse Deer spotted a snoozing snake dangling from a nearby branch.

Mouse Deer said, "I was wrong to trick you, but I must ask that you spare my life. I am on very important business guarding the king's magic belt." Mouse Deer pointed at the snake.

"When you put it like that, I feel I have no choice but to let you try the royal cake," said Mouse Deer. "But before you begin, please let me run away, so I can hide from the king. He will be so angry with me, I fear for my life."

The tiger agreed, and Mouse Deer darted quickly into the trees, ducking through the undergrowth and leaping over obstacles until she came to a hiding place far away from the tiger.

When Mouse Deer disappeared into the trees, the tiger stooped to take a big bite from the special royal cake. Imagine his horror when he found that it was actually a big pat of buffalo

"What nonsense!" snarled the tiger.

"It's not nonsense!" protested Mouse Deer. "Whenever the king wears this special belt, he can make a wish. The king was here just now, and I saw him use it with my own eyes."

"What kind of wishes can he make?" asked the tiger, his curiosity aroused.

"He can wish for anything! It's a magic belt—the only one in the world."

The hungry tiger imagined what he would ask for if he had a magic belt like the king's, and his mouth watered at the thought of fresh meat.

"Forgive me for being a little bad-tempered earlier," said the tiger. "I don't know what came over me."

"You are forgiven," smiled Mouse Deer, guessing that the tiger had fallen for her story again.

"Perhaps I could try the magic belt?" said the tiger.

Mouse Deer looked shocked. "Never! Only the king can wear it!"

"If you let me try it, I promise I won't be mean to you ever again," pleaded the tiger. "I won't even try to hunt you."

"But the king will be enraged if I let you wear his belt. He will execute me!"

"Then we just won't tell him!" smiled the tiger. "He will never know!"

"Oh, but the king knows everything," said Mouse Deer, sounding nervous. "I know. Why don't you let me run away? I'll tell the king I was attacked. Then he won't punish me if he finds out you tried on his magic belt."

"Good idea—run along!" said the tiger, eager to slip on the magic belt and wish himself a huge feast.

~~~~~~~~~~~~~~~~

Mouse Deer ran into the trees and hid herself well.

"Ha!" said the tiger. "The king's magic belt is all mine now!"

He swiped at the belt with his paw. But just as he did so, the snoozy snake woke up and was alarmed to find itself wrapped around the body of a big cat.

Thinking the tiger was planning to eat it, the snake coiled its body tightly around the tiger's neck and squeezed hard.

"Ow!" yelped the tiger, gasping for air. "You aren't a belt—you're a snake!"

The snake hissed, and the tiger struggled until, at last, he broke free. The angry snake, annoyed that its afternoon nap had been disturbed, slithered into the undergrowth, and the angry tiger let out a mighty roar that was heard for miles around:

"I'LL GET YOU, MOUSE DEER!"

But he didn't—Mouse Deer was much too clever for him!

The Sword in the Stone

There was once a great king of England called Uther Pendragon, who, with his fair wife Igraine, ruled the land in a time of troublesome noblemen and lords.

In the most troubled of times, they had a baby boy, and they named him Arthur. The king and queen were delighted, but King Uther's advisor, the wise old wizard, Merlin, had a vision that the young heir's life was in danger. He urged the king to keep his son's birth a secret and send him away.

With a heavy heart, the king agreed, and Merlin took baby Arthur to the great knight, Sir Ector, where the child grew up as his adopted son and half-brother to Sir Kay.

Arthur never knew that he had royal blood, and Sir Ector had no idea that he was raising the king's son.

Arthur grew up to be a generous, kind, and valiant young man, but because he was thought to come from a lowly background, he could never be a knight like Sir Ector and Sir Kay. Instead, he served them loyally.

When Arthur was sixteen, King Uther became ill and died. Without a known heir to replace him on the throne and lead the country, England fell into great unrest. Fighting broke out across the country as rival lords battled for the right to rule over the land.

Desperate to end the country's turmoil, Merlin the wizard came up with a cunning plan.

In the courtyard of Westminster Abbey, Merlin placed a large marble stone. He stood an iron anvil on top of it and embedded

a magnificent enchanted sword deep inside it. Along the sword's blade, an inscription read:

"Whoso pulleth out this sword from this stone is the rightful King of England."

He then summoned all the lords and noblemen to London for a grand tournament and invited them to pull the sword from the stone.

Merlin knew, of course, that Sir Ector and his son Sir Kay would come—and bring young Arthur with them.

The tournament took place on New Year's Day, and there was jousting, feasting, and dancing to look forward to—but the thing that got everyone excited was the thought of pulling the enchanted sword from the stone and winning the throne of England.

Sir Ector and Sir Kay set out on the long ride to London, with Arthur in tow. But as they neared Westminster Abbey, Sir Kay remembered that he had left his best sword at home.

"Fear not, brother," said Arthur. "You will not be without your sword today. I will make sure of that!"

However, Arthur knew it would be impossible for him to ride all the way home and get back in time for the day's events, so he set out to look for an alternative.

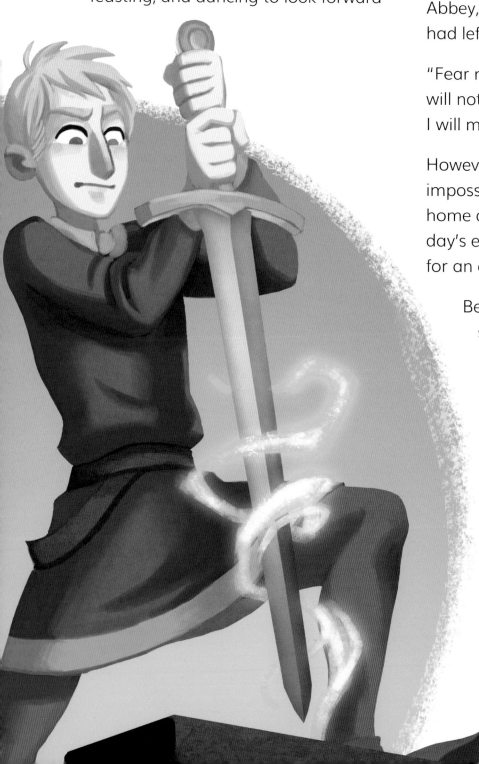

Before long, he spotted a sword sticking out of an anvil outside Westminster Abbey.

"Perfect!" smiled Arthur, and he clambered on top of the marble stone, gripped the hilt of the sword, and slid it out of the anvil as if it were a knife in butter.

As quickly as he could, Arthur rode back to Sir Kay and presented the sword to him.

As soon as Sir Kay saw it, he knew what it was. "Father!" he exclaimed. "I have the sword in the stone. I am the true King of England!"

But Sir Ector had been trusted with Arthur's life for a reason—he was a wise and honest man.

"Tell me the truth, son," he said. "Where did you get this sword?"

Sir Kay hesitated and then admitted that Arthur had given it to him.

Sir Ector turned to Arthur. "How did you get this sword, Arthur?"

"I took it from the stone outside the Abbey, sir," said Arthur, hanging his head in shame.

"Were there any knights present at the time?" asked Sir Ector.

"No, sir."

"And was the sword lying by the stone?"

"No, sir. I pulled it from an anvil."

Sir Ector raised his eyebrows in disbelief.

"Show me how you did it, Arthur."

So Arthur led Sir Ector and Sir Kay back to the marble stone, where Sir Ector plunged the sword back into the anvil. Quite a crowd had gathered by now, as someone had noticed that the sword was missing.

To test his strength, Sir Ector pulled and tugged at the sword with all his might, but it could not be moved.

Sir Kay stepped forward and tried his luck, too, but for all his heaving and wrenching, the sword wouldn't budge.

At last, Arthur came forward. Once more, he gripped the sword, and it slid from the stone without any effort at all.

At this, the crowd gasped, and Sir Ector and Sir Kay fell to their knees before the bewildered young lad.

"What are you doing, Father?" asked Arthur, feeling confused.

"We are bowing before the one true king of England, sire," said Sir Ector.

"Only the true king can pull the enchanted sword from the stone."

As Arthur read the sword's inscription for the first time, Sir Ector explained that he had never known the identity of Arthur's real father. Just then, Merlin the wizard pushed his way through the heaving crowd to stand by Arthur.

"All hail the only son of King Uther Pendragon!" cried Merlin, raising Arthur's hand and the enchanted sword in the air.

"All hail King Arthur!" shouted Sir Ector, and the crowd cheered wildly for their new king.

And so, in an instant, Arthur's life changed completely, and a few days later, he was crowned King of England.

As Merlin knew he would be, Arthur made a good and brave king. With the wizard as his advisor and his trusty sword at his side, he led the country into a time of great peace and happiness—and he was much loved by his people.

The Lucky Pedlar

Long ago, in a small village in Norfolk, England, there lived a pedlar, who went around selling goods from door to door. Times were hard where he lived, and people had little money to spare, so no matter how hard and how long the pedlar worked, he never seemed to have enough food to put on the table.

One night, he went to bed with a rumbling tummy, and he had a dream so strong and vivid that the next day, it was all he could think about. In the dream, a wise man told him that if he journeyed to London Bridge and stood there for three days, he would receive wonderful news that would change his life forever.

The pedlar tried to forget the dream and go about his business, but it came to him again that night and also the next. Each time, the dream seemed clearer and brighter. Soon, the pedlar could think of nothing else. Finally, he decided to set out for London to see if his dream would come true.

He arrived at London Bridge at sunrise, and though he was weary, the pedlar stood on the bridge, in the middle of the hustle and bustle, with a hopeful look on his face. A whole day passed, and nothing happened, but the pedlar didn't give up. He stood there for a second day and a third, hoping for good news.

Now it happened that a shopkeeper had spotted the pedlar in the middle of the bridge and was baffled by this strange man who stood there, day after day, for no reason. Unable to contain his curiosity, the shopkeeper asked the pedlar why he was there. The pedlar told him about his dream.

The shopkeeper laughed heartily and patted the pedlar on the back.

"Let me tell you, good fellow, last night, I dreamt of a small village in Norfolk that I have never visited. In the dream, there was a poor pedlar's house with a mighty oak tree behind it, and hidden

beneath the tree was a vast treasure! Now do you think I'd be such a fool to travel so far to see if that dream was true? No, I'm too wise for that! Waste no more time, sir, and go home!"

The pedlar could barely contain his joy, because even though the shopkeeper thought he was a fool, he knew that there was indeed a mighty oak tree behind his house in Norfolk. This was the good news he had been waiting for! He set off for home as quickly as he could.

When he got there, he didn't waste a second in starting to dig under the oak tree. It didn't take long before his spade hit something hard. The pedlar leaned deep into the hole and hauled out a small wooden chest. He was delighted to see that it was full of golden coins! When he looked more closely, the pedlar saw that it also had some intricate words carved on the lid:

Dig again where I stood,
Find something that's twice as good!

The pedlar dug down deeper still, until he found another wooden chest much larger than the first. When he heaved it out, he was astonished to find that it was crammed with even more gold coins. He was no fool at all—the lucky pedlar's dream had come true!

Immediately, he shared his good fortune among his friends, and he set to work helping to rebuild the village into a much nicer place for everyone to live in. Today, there is a real church in Norfolk with a beautiful wooden carving in it of that generous and lucky pedlar.

The Magic Harp

There once was a man named Taffy Morgan, who was one of the few men in Wales who didn't have a beautiful singing voice. He couldn't sing or play an instrument, and worst of all, he thought he could! His friends and family would cover their ears whenever Taffy was making music—and Taffy liked to make music a lot!

One day, a famous bard, well known for his wonderful music and poems, walked by Taffy's house and heard him playing his old harp. Taffy's friend asked the bard what he thought of the music. "That's music?" said the bard. "It's the worst racket I've ever heard!"

The bard and the friend laughed, but Taffy had heard everything. His feelings were hurt—because he loved to play his harp more than anything.

The next day, Taffy was busy humming a little ditty when there was a knock on his door. Three beautiful strangers stood on his doorstep.

"Sir, we are hungry and thirsty. Please could you spare us a drink and a morsel to eat?"

"Of course!" said Taffy. He invited them in and served them home-baked bread, cheese, and a large jug of milk. "Please help yourselves, friends!"

As the three strangers sat at the table, Taffy decided to entertain them with a cheerful tune or two. He sang and plucked away at his old harp, and to his surprise, the strangers seemed to enjoy it. They happily ate their food and clapped along with his music.

When they had finished, they got up to leave, and one of the strangers said to Taffy, "Thank you for your kindness! We are not ordinary visitors—we are fairy folk, and we would like to reward you with a wish. What would you like, sir?"

Taffy couldn't believe his luck! He thought for a moment and said, "If you please, I would like a harp that, no matter how badly I play, makes merry tunes and pleases all who hear it."

"It is yours!" said the fairies. There was a bright flash of light and there, in the middle of the room, stood a shining golden harp! The three fairies thanked Taffy again and said goodbye.

Taffy pulled up a stool and sat next to the harp. He swept his hands across the strings and began to pluck a simple tune. As soon as he touched it, the notes rang out bright and clear, making a melody much better than anything Taffy could ever play. The magic harp's music floated through the open window and drifted all around the village.

Taffy's friend was unable to resist the wonderful melody, and he dashed into Taffy's house. He soon started laughing and dancing around the room. His wife and several of Taffy's other friends followed him. Pretty soon, the room was full of villagers, all smiling and dancing happy jigs. This went on for many hours, and all the time, the dancers seemed to grow merrier and more energetic.

When Taffy stopped playing, the dancers remarked how they all felt better than ever! News spread quickly of Taffy's amazing harp-playing, and by the following night, the whole village had gathered around Taffy's house to hear him play.

Taffy played the harp again, and it was even livelier than before. The moment he touched the strings, a brilliant melody began, and everyone in the crowd danced. Even some of the old folk who couldn't walk very well found themselves whirling around Taffy's house. As long as he played, people danced, and because Taffy enjoyed playing so much, the grass around his home was soon worn away from all the jiving, jigging, and jumping. The effect of the magic harp was so strong, that when Taffy stopped playing, everyone felt young again. It was a miracle!

That night, many people offered Taffy lots of money to play his harp for them, and some even wanted to buy his harp, but Taffy didn't want money; he was happy just to be able to play music that people enjoyed for once.

And so it went on, every night for a week, until people were coming to visit from far and wide to join in the dance. Even the bard, who thought that Taffy was a terrible musician, came to see what all the fuss was about.

Taffy spotted the bard by his door and decided to get his revenge. He plucked the harp harder, and the song that came out was fast, loud, and wild. The bard couldn't stop himself from joining in—his heels began to kick, and his arms waved in the air. He and the crowd became swept up in a quick, swirling dance and soon started to spin out of control. Suddenly, the bard hit himself hard against the wall.

"Ha!" thought Taffy. "That serves you right for being mean to me!" He kept on playing, while the bard grew dizzy from all the spinning and the jigging and the banging into things. Taffy played on, even when the bard begged him to stop. By now, the music was so fast that dancers were dropping to the floor, exhausted.

Eventually, the bard's legs gave way, and he collapsed in a heap, too. Taffy laughed so hard, he stopped playing, but the moment he took his hands off the strings, the fairy visitors appeared. They were very cross with Taffy, as he had used their gift to get revenge. In fact, they were so unhappy that they took his magical harp away from him! Taffy was disappointed, but he knew that he deserved it.

From then on, Taffy never sang or played a note of music again— and the whole village was thankful for the peace and quiet!

Maui Goes Fishing

Maui's four older brothers never let him join in their fun. One morning, they all rose with the sun to go deep-sea fishing in their special canoe.

"Please let me come with you," begged Maui, but his older brothers just laughed at him and teased him. "One day, little one, but not today. There isn't enough room in our canoe for you as well as all the fish we're planning to bring home with us. Another time, perhaps!"

But Maui wasn't one to sulk. He had magic powers that his family didn't know about. While his brothers got their fishing tackle ready, he came up with a plan to use his magic. When he was a baby, he had been given an enchanted jawbone by the ocean spirits. He hid it in a secret box.

He took out the jawbone and crafted it into a fishing hook, then he braided flax into a fishing line, and he climbed into the bottom of their canoe, concealing himself inside a basket.

When at last the four brothers were ready to set out, they grumbled about how much heavier the canoe felt but set off over the waves to a place where the water was teeming with life.

When they were far out at sea, one of the brothers grabbed the basket to store his catch inside—and uncovered Maui. "Little squirt!" he said. "You tricked us! We're taking you back to shore right now!"

The brothers took up their paddles again, but Maui wished on his magic hook that the seashore would look farther and farther away—and after ten minutes of paddling, the brothers were so tired, they gave up.

"Keep out of our way, pipsqueak," they grumbled, and the brothers cast their fishing lines into the sea.

Maui stayed down at the bottom end of the canoe, sure that his brothers would be so busy catching fish, they wouldn't know what he was up to—then he quietly dropped the mystical hook over the edge of the boat.

At the other end of the canoe, the brothers were having great success, and their basket was starting to fill up with fish. But all of a sudden, Maui felt a powerful tug on his line. The tug was so strong that Maui feared he might be dragged into the water.

"Brothers! Quick, help me!" he cried, gripping his fishing line tightly. The four brothers dashed toward Maui just as the canoe was about to capsize, and together, they heaved and tugged with all their might until—to their great surprise—a towering hunk of land surfaced before them. It was shaped like a fish. Maui had caught New Zealand's North Island!

Maui was worried that the ocean spirits would be angry with him for catching the island, so he dived into the sea to ask for their forgiveness. Before he went, he asked his brothers to guard his brilliant catch.

However, while Maui was making peace, his greedy brothers started to hack and chop at the fish-shaped land, trying to claim little bits of it for themselves—and this is why New Zealand's North Island is so craggy and mountainous.

After performing the miracle of fishing out North Island, Maui became famous among the Maori people, and he grew up to be a much-loved demigod. And to this day, the North Island of New Zealand is also known as Te Ika A Maui—or Maui's Fish.

How Rabbit Got Long Ears

Many moons ago, when the Earth was still quite young, Rabbit's ears weren't at all like they are today—they were rather short and stumpy.

Short-eared Rabbit was well known throughout the woods for playing tricks on everyone—and today was no exception. It was a warm, sunny day, but Rabbit was fidgety and had nothing to do. He was feeling rather bored, so he decided to cause a little mischief with his friends.

First, he went to the pond to find his friend, Beaver. "Thank goodness I found you!" cried Rabbit, sounding flustered.

"We must hurry and hunt for all the food we can find, or we'll all starve!"

"Did you hear the news?" Rabbit asked. "They say that the sun is never going to rise again!"

"What?" said Beaver. "Who told you?" But Rabbit didn't hear—he was already hopping away, grinning to himself. "He must be going to warn the other animals," thought Beaver.

Beaver was very upset to hear such bad news and was looking downright gloomy when Squirrel scurried by.

"What's the problem, old chum?" enquired Squirrel.

"Didn't you hear?" sighed Beaver. "The sun is never going to rise again! Oh woe is me, oh woe is me!"

Then Beaver scampered into his lodge, clutching a large supply of pondweed in his paws.

Squirrel quickly scampered off to tell Chipmunk, Chipmunk woke up Raccoon to tell him, Raccoon told Bear and so on—until all the animals in the woods had heard the news of the disappearing sun. They were all very worried indeed.

"If the sun never rises again," sniffled Squirrel, "then it will be dark and cold all the time—even worse than winter! We must hurry and hunt for all the food we can find, or we'll all starve!"

So the animals ran off in different directions—and instead of playing or relaxing in the hazy sunshine, they hunted for food. Bear piled as many blueberries as he could fit into his paws, and Squirrel scrambled around foraging for nuts. Everybody felt sad that summer was about to end.

Everybody except for Rabbit, who was hiding in the bushes chuckling at his friends, getting ready for the sun to disappear. Rabbit thought this was his best trick yet.

Then along came Glooscap. He was the first human, and legend had it that he was made from a bolt of lightning. The animals loved Glooscap, and they always ran to his side, but today, as he walked by, they didn't even look up. Instead, they were rushing back and forth, looking worried.

"Bear!" said Glooscap, glad to see his friend. "Why are you so busy?"

Bear hurried by. "Can't talk now!" he said. "I don't have time!"

Glooscap walked on, but none of his animal friends looked up and said hello.

"Raccoon!" said Glooscap. "How are you today? Enjoying the sunshine?"

Raccoon gave a panicked squeal and darted toward his den carrying an armful of acorns.

Glooscap quickly strode up to Bear. "What is wrong with you all?" he demanded. "Why is everybody looking so troubled?"

"Haven't you heard?" said Bear. "The sun isn't going to rise again! We have to gather food quickly and get ready for winter, or we'll all starve!"

Glooscap couldn't believe what he was hearing. "What nonsense!" he said. "Who told you such a thing?" But Bear just kept on gathering berries.

Glooscap decided to summon all the animals and get to the bottom of this strange story about the sun. They sat around him in a circle, many with their foraged food in their paws.

"Who told you about the sun, Bear?"

"Raccoon told me," said Bear.

Then Raccoon said, "Well, Chipmunk told me about it!"

One by one, the animals revealed who had told them the story of the sun, all the way back to Beaver, who said, "It was Rabbit who told me!"

Glooscap knew that Rabbit was the only animal missing from the circle. "Where is Rabbit?" he asked.

"I bet he's hiding!" said Beaver, who had guessed by now that he had fallen for another of Rabbit's tricks.

Beaver was right—Rabbit knew his joke had gone too far this time, so he was nervously hiding in the bushes.

Glooscap searched the woods until he found Rabbit's hiding place.

When he saw Rabbit, he grabbed him by his short ears, lifted him up, and held him there for a very long time, while he gave him a good telling off for playing such a mean trick.

Glooscap made Rabbit say "sorry" to his friends, and as he did so, Rabbit's little ears stretched and stretched ...

... and that is how Rabbit got his long ears.

The Ant and the Grasshopper

It was a beautiful summer's day in the cornfield, and Grasshopper was having the best time, leaning back on a stalk, chirping away, and making his sweet grasshopper music.

Occasionally, Grasshopper would stop, hop over to another stalk of corn, stretch out his wings, then start all over again.

"Happy days!" he thought.

Just then, he saw an ant passing by, carrying a plump kernel of corn on her back. The ant was huffing and puffing under the weight of her load.

Grasshopper stopped playing music and called, "Hey, Ant! What's the big hurry? Why don't you lie back in the sunshine for a while and listen to some of my music?"

"Can't stop!" huffed the ant. "Got to get this to the ant hill!"

"But I've seen you pass by five times today already!" laughed Grasshopper. "Surely you have enough food for your dinner by now?"

"It's not for dinner!" puffed the ant. "It's for winter!" And she struggled on with her heavy load.

"Winter!" exclaimed Grasshopper. "But it's a bright sunny day—perfect for lazing around—and there is food all around us! Why worry about winter now?" he asked.

The ant stopped for a second.

"Summer doesn't last forever, you know! We have to build our stores

He decided to find somewhere to spend winter.

for winter and prepare our nest, so that we don't freeze or starve—and you should be doing the same!"

The ant shook her head at the lazy grasshopper and went on her way.

Grasshopper just laughed at her. "Ha! Winter, indeed! Those ants just don't know how to have fun!" And he relaxed on his stalk and started to chirp and play even louder music.

The ant passed by the Grasshopper three more times that day, and each time, the ant shook her head at him, and the Grasshopper waved and continued chirping until the sun went down. The same happened the next day and for many days after that.

Soon, the summer sun faded, and it started to turn bitterly cold in the cornfield—winter was on its way.

One morning, Grasshopper woke up to find a thick, sharp frost everywhere. The corn had withered and died in the frost, and Grasshopper shivered so much, he couldn't even chirp.

"No more lazy days in the sunshine," he thought sadly, and he decided to find somewhere to spend the winter.

But as he made his way across the cornfield, he found that every tiny nook and cranny had already been taken—all the other insects and animals had arrived there first.

As the day wore on, the air grew icier, and Grasshopper couldn't find anything to eat. He was cold and tired, and his tummy was rumbling.

Eventually, he came to an anthill. It looked warm and snug inside, and through a little window, he could see the busy ant he had met in the summer serving some delicious corn to her friends and family.

Shivering, Grasshopper knocked at her door. The ant answered, and he asked, "Please, dear ant, can you spare me some corn?"

"Didn't I warn you?" said the ant. "While you were lazing about in the sun making music, I was working hard so I wouldn't go hungry this winter."

Though the ant was annoyed with Grasshopper for being so lazy, she wasn't unkind—she gave him some corn and sent him on his way.

Grasshopper knew then that he should have listened to what the wise little ant had said. That winter he learned a very hard lesson ...

Always be prepared!

The Gingerbread Man

Once upon a time, a little old lady and a little old man lived together in a little old house on a hill. They had lived there for a long and happy time together.

One day, the little old lady decided to bake a gingerbread man as a special treat for her husband. She carefully kneaded the dough, rolled it out, and cut out the perfect shape. She gave the gingerbread man currants for its eyes and its nose, and put it in the oven to bake.

When the little old house was filled with the sweet aroma of warm ginger, she knew that the gingerbread man must be ready. But when she opened the oven door to take it out, she got quite a surprise. The gingerbread man stood up, leaped out of the oven, and ran across the floor at great speed toward the kitchen door!

The old man, who had been looking forward to this tasty treat very much, chased after him, shouting "Hey! Stop, Gingerbread Man! You look good enough to eat!"

But the Gingerbread Man just laughed and said:

"Run, run, as fast as you can! You can't catch me, I'm the Gingerbread Man!"

And off he dashed, through the door and down the garden path. The old man and the old lady tried their best to catch up, but they just weren't quick enough. The Gingerbread Man ran through the gate and down the lane, where a big hairy sheepdog was blocking his path.

The sheepdog thought that the Gingerbread Man smelled quite delicious. "Mmmm ... Don't run away, Gingerbread Man!" woofed the sheepdog. "You look good enough to eat!"

But the Gingerbread Man just laughed and said:

"I ran away from the old lady and the old man, and I can run away from you! **Run, run as fast as you can! You can't catch me, I'm the Gingerbread Man!"**

The hungry sheepdog chased after him, but the Gingerbread Man darted through a small hole in a hedge and disappeared.

The Gingerbread Man ran across a meadow, all the time chuckling to himself. He soon came to a black cow grazing on some daisies.

When the cow saw him coming, she licked her lips. "Mmmm ... Don't rush off, Gingerbread Man!" she mooed. "You look good enough to eat!"

But the Gingerbread Man just laughed and said:

"I ran away from the old lady, the old man, and the big hairy sheepdog, and I can run away from you! **Run, run as fast as you can! You can't catch me, I'm the Gingerbread Man!"**

The cow wasn't a very fast runner, so the Gingerbread Man soon got away. Off he went again, across the meadow and into the pasture, where he found a brown horse munching on some hay.

The horse's tummy rumbled when it saw the Gingerbread Man. "Mmmm ... Don't dash, Gingerbread Man!" neighed the horse. "You look good enough to eat!"

But the Gingerbread Man just laughed and said:

"I ran away from the old lady, the old man, the big hairy sheepdog, and the black cow, and I can run away from you!"

"Run, run as fast as you can! catch me, I'm the

You can't
Gingerbread Man!"

With that, the Gingerbread Man darted through the horse's legs and to the other side of the pasture. The horse galloped after him, but the Gingerbread Man was just too fast.

⸕⸕⸕⸕⸕⸕⸕⸕⸕⸕⸕⸕⸕

Soon, the Gingerbread Man reached the river, where he found a fox sitting by the water's edge. The Gingerbread Man wanted to get to the other side, but he knew he couldn't swim there, or he'd get terribly soggy.

"You're very fast!" said the fox, sniffing at the sweet gingerbread. "Who are you running away from?"

"I ran away from the old lady, the old man, the big hairy sheepdog, the black cow, and the brown horse, and I can run away from you, too!" said the Gingerbread Man proudly.

"Why would you run away from me? I'm not chasing you," said the fox. "Anyway, who else will take you to the other side of the river?"

The fox stood up lazily and walked into the water. "Jump onto my tail," he said to the Gingerbread Man, "and I'll ferry you across."

The Gingerbread Man stepped onto the fox's bushy tail, and the fox began to paddle across the wide river.

They hadn't gone very far when the fox turned his head and said, "Gingerbread Man, you're too heavy for my tail. I'm afraid you'll slide off. Why don't you jump onto my back instead?" So the Gingerbread Man jumped onto the fox's back.

The fox swam a little more, then he turned again and said, "Gingerbread Man, the water is getting deep. I'm afraid you'll get wet. Why don't you step onto my shoulder instead?" So the Gingerbread Man climbed up onto the fox's shoulder.

The fox swam some more, then he said, "Gingerbread Man, the water is getting deeper again. I'm afraid you'll get splashed. Why don't you stand on the end of my nose?" So the Gingerbread Man carefully tiptoed onto his nose.

They paddled for a little while longer, and just as the fox reached the other side of the river, he opened his mouth wide and bit off the Gingerbread Man's leg!

"Oh dear!" said the Gingerbread Man. "I'm a quarter gone!"

The fox took another bite, and the Gingerbread Man said, "Oh dear! I'm half gone!"

Then the fox bit off both of the Gingerbread Man's arms, and he said, "Oh dear! I'm three-quarters gone!"

Then, before he knew it, the sly fox gobbled him all up, and the Gingerbread Man said, "Oh dear! I'm all gone!"

And that was the end of the Gingerbread Man!

The Mouse Merchant

In a small Indian town, there a lived a boy and his poor widowed mother. Though they hadn't a penny to their name, the boy's mother had done her best to give her son a good education.

On the boy's thirteenth birthday, his mother said, "Son, when your father was alive, he was a merchant, and it is time for you to follow in his footsteps. There is a rich merchant named Visakhila who lives in the next town. He is known for lending money to poor men who want to make better lives for themselves. Please go to him, and ask for a loan to get you started."

The boy was excited at the thought of being a merchant like his father, so he set off without delay.

When he arrived at Visakhila's house, he heard an angry voice shout, "I gave you many rupees, and you have simply wasted them all! Do you see that dead mouse on the floor? Someone with intelligence could take even that and turn it into money!"

At that, the boy stepped into the room and said, "I accept your challenge! I will take that mouse as my loan from you!" He put it in his pocket and wrote out a receipt for the merchant.

The merchant and the young man he had been scolding both looked on in shock and then burst into laughter. However, when the boy left, the merchant put the receipt in his safe.

As he walked down the road, the boy met a market trader who was being clawed by a fidgety cat. "I'll give you this dead mouse to your cat to play with, in exchange for some goods from your stall," said the boy. The market trader was so grateful, he gave the boy two large handfuls of chickpea flour and a pitcher.

The boy used the chickpea flour to make delicious flatbreads, and he filled the pitcher with spring water. Then he set himself up in a shady spot on the road between the forest and the town gates.

At the end of the day, many hungry, thirsty woodcutters came out of the forest, and the boy offered them some flatbreads and water. In return, each woodcutter gave him some wood.

The next day, the boy sold some of his wood at the market to buy more flour to make flatbreads. He stored the rest of the rupees in his purse.

He did this for many weeks until he had built up a huge supply of wood, and his purse was filled with money.

When an unexpected cold spell arrived and people were shivering in their homes, the boy was able to sell all of the wood he had stored for a very great price.

Now he had enough money to set himself up as a merchant, with his own shop and even a room for his mother to live in. With hard work, honesty, and intelligence, the boy soon grew into a wealthy young man, and customers came from far and wide to buy his goods.

One day, when he knew that he had truly made his fortune, he visited the goldsmith and asked him to make a mouse of solid gold. The young man delivered the golden mouse to Visakhila to repay his debt.

At first, Visakhila was confused, but then he remembered the old receipt at the back of his safe, and the boy who had once picked up a dead mouse from his floor. Visakhila laughed and congratulated the young man on his success who, from that day on, became famous throughout India as the Mouse Merchant!

The Four Dragons

Many thousands of years ago, the great country of China had no rivers or lakes—just the sea on one side and the rain that fell from the sky.

In that precious sea lived four mighty dragons named Long Dragon, Yellow Dragon, Pearl Dragon, and Black Dragon. They all served the Jade Emperor, who lived in the heavens above, and it was their job to look after the people of China as they sailed and fished in the sea.

All was well until the Jade Emperor fell in love with a fairy enchantress. The Emperor became so bewitched by her that he completely forgot his duties—including making the rain fall on the crops below. Harvests quickly withered and died, and the people of China started to go hungry. They prayed to the Jade Emperor for help.

"Dear Emperor!" they begged, on their hands and knees. "We have not a grain of rice to eat! Please send us some rain before we all starve!" But the Emperor didn't hear them.

It pained the four dragons to see the people suffer so much, so they flew to the Jade Emperor's heavenly palace. When they entered his court, they found him being entertained by the fairy. He was totally entranced.

When he saw the dragons, he cried, "What are you doing here? Shouldn't you be guarding the sea?"

"Dear Emperor," bowed Long Dragon, "the crops are dying, and the people are hungry. We beg you to send some rain before everyone starves!"

"Very well," sighed the Jade Emperor, and he waved them away. "Go back to your watery home, and I will send some rain tomorrow."

The dragons thanked him, and he went back to listening to his fairy music with a faraway look in his eyes.

The next day came, and not a drop of rain fell from the sky. The same happened the following day and the day after that. The people became truly desperate, and the four dragons couldn't bear to hear their cries.

"The Jade Emperor will surely punish us for doing his job," said Pearl Dragon, "but we must save these people before it is too late!"

"Aren't we the dragons of the sea?" cried Black Dragon. "Let us carry as much water as we can and fill the clouds with it!"

"We must hurry," urged Yellow Dragon. "We don't have much time!"

And so the four dragons dived into the sea and swallowed as much water as they could hold in their jaws. Then they flew into the sky and sprayed the seawater into the clouds. They kept on doing this until the clouds were ready to burst, and rain began to pour down heavily on the land below.

The people of China rejoiced to see the rain and cheered so loudly that they awoke the Jade Emperor from his fairy entertainment. He looked down from his palace, and when he saw what the four dragons were doing, he flew into a fearsome rage.

"How dare the dragons make it rain without my permission!" he shouted.

The Jade Emperor sent his strongest guards to capture the four dragons, and they were dragged to his palace for punishment.

Though the dragons pleaded and explained how desperate the people had been, the Jade Emperor was so angered and insulted by their actions that he refused to listen to them and threw them in prison.

That night, the Emperor called for the God of Mountains and asked him to bring his four largest mountains.

"When you have them," demanded the Emperor, "place one mountain on top of each dragon, so that they may never escape or disobey me again!"

The God of Mountains used his powers to make four giant mountains appear, floating in the air. He placed one on top of each of the four dragons, trapping them for eternity.

When the Emperor was satisfied, the God of Mountains sent the peaks back to where they belonged, with the dragons imprisoned inside them.

But the four dragons were determined to protect the people, so they changed themselves into rivers, rushing down from their mountain prisons, filling the dry gorges, watering the fields, and flowing out to the sea. And this is how China's four greatest rivers came to be.

In the far south, the Pearl Dragon flowed out to the sea as the Zhujiang (Pearl River); in the south, the Long Dragon became the Yangtze (Long River); in central China, the Yellow Dragon turned into the Huanghe (Yellow River); and farther north, the Black Dragon transformed itself into the Heilongjiang (Black River).

From that day on, whenever the Jade Emperor lost interest in the people he was supposed to care for, nobody had to suffer, because the four dragon rivers were always there to provide water for them.

The Wise Bear

One pleasant afternoon, two friends were walking through the forest on their way to spend a weekend camping together.

The friends had known each other since they were little children and had grown up together, but they hadn't seen each other for a long time. They were both looking forward to their break and a chance to catch up with each other's news. But just when they reached the thickest part of the forest, a huge brown bear strolled onto the path before them.

One of the friends, who spotted the bear first, panicked and ran into the forest. Without a second to think, he found the nearest large tree, and he scrambled up it as quickly as he could, hiding himself among the branches.

The other friend, who was left all alone, was certain he would be attacked and killed by the bear. Not sure what to do, he dropped to the ground, and though he was shaking with fear, he tried to stay as still as a statue.

From the top of his tree, the first friend saw what had happened and thought his friend must have fainted with fright.

The brown bear waddled up to the fallen friend and sniffed around him, then he nudged his body with his giant paw and pushed at him with his big, wet snout.

The friend was terrified, but he managed to stay still. When the bear's snout came near his face, he held his breath for as long as he could, so that the bear would think he was dead. All this time, the friend up the tree stayed quiet.

At last, the bear gave up. He straightened up and started to waddle away. The friend on the ground let out a sigh of relief, but suddenly, the bear turned around and came back! He leaned down to the frightened friend and seemed to whisper something in his ear. Then the bear stood up and lumbered off into the trees.

~~~~~~~~~~

The friend who had scurried up the tree trunk waited until he was sure that it was safe to come down. When he saw his old friend shakily climb to his feet, he clambered down the tree and joined the forest path again.

"Phew!" he laughed. "That was very close. I thought you were in trouble for a second!"

"Yes," said his friend, still a little shaken.

"You know, it's weird. It looked like the bear leaned down to whisper something to you."

"He did!" said his friend, looking thoughtful.

"Really? The bear spoke! What did he say?"

"He said ... never go camping with a friend who abandons you at the first sign of danger."

And with that, the friend who the bear had spoken to picked up his rucksack, turned around, and headed for home again.

Finn MacCool

Many hundreds of years ago, the north of Ireland was home to a giant known as Finn MacCool. Despite his large size and huge strength, MacCool was a kind giant, who enjoyed living peacefully with his wife, Oonagh.

However, he had one great rival who lived across the sea in Scotland—his name was Benandonner, the Red Man. Benandonner spent all day and night shouting insults across the waves at Finn MacCool, until one morning, MacCool decided he could take no more. He broke off some rocks and started throwing them into the sea to build a pathway across the sea to Scotland. When he had finished, he was quite exhausted, but he yelled at Benandonner to come to Ireland and fight him once and for all!

However, when mighty Finn MacCool caught sight of Benandonner in the distance, he saw that the Scottish giant

was twice his size! Though MacCool could easily fit fifty men in his hands, Benandonner looked like he could lift a hundred or more! MacCool regretted picking a fight, and he ran home to his clever wife, Oonagh, who always knew what to do.

"Quick as you like, now," she urged her husband. "Go and tear down two trees, and fetch your hatchet, some nails, and your hammer!"

MacCool dashed outside and tore two trees out of the hillside, then he presented them to Oonagh.

"Now, carve a sharp point in the end of one tree, and cut the other tree into long planks. When you've finished, lean the pointed tree against the wall, and nail the planks to our bed to look like a cradle."

MacCool was puzzled, but he knew it was wise to do as his wife said.

"Right, get into the bed now, and I'll wrap the blankets around you and a sheet around your head. You need to pretend you're a baby!"

MacCool curled up in the cradle and sucked his thumb!

"Close your eyes," Oonagh told him, "and when you hear Benandonner sit down, let out a big wail!"

Soon enough, Finn MacCool heard the thumping steps of Benandonner coming toward his fort, followed by the thud of a heavy fist on the door.

Oonagh opened the door and said in a stern voice, "Well, now! There's no need to bang so hard—you'll wake the baby! If it's Finn you're after, then he's out hunting, but you can come in and wait if you like."

Benandonner entered the great hall, and Oonagh said, "Would you like to put your spear next to my husband's?"

She pointed at the tree with the sharp end, and Benandonner was startled to see its size. He put his smaller spear right next to it, then sat down heavily on the bench, nervously crushing a boulder between his fingers. At this, Finn MacCool wailed like a baby.

"Oh dear," said Oonagh. "The baby must be hungry. I've made some griddle cakes; would you like some?" And she offered some to her guest.

"Irish giants are famous for their very strong teeth."

Benandonner accepted, but when he bit down on his griddle cake, he chipped his two front teeth, because Oonagh had hidden an iron plate in it!

"Whatever's wrong with you?" she exclaimed. "Why, my husband eats these all the time. Even the baby eats them!" She gave Finn, disguised as a baby, a griddle cake without an iron plate hidden inside. Benandonner saw the baby eat it without any trouble, and he started to feel most worried.

"Sure enough," said Oonagh. "Irish giants are famous for their very strong teeth. Didn't you know? You should come over here and feel them!"

Benandonner approached the cradle, and was horrified when he saw the size of the baby in it. He cautiously put his finger by the baby's mouth to feel its teeth, and Finn MacCool bit down on it as hard as he could.

Benandonner jumped back, roaring in pain. "Goodness," he thought. "If the baby is this big and strong, how gigantic must his father be?"

Terrified at the idea of fighting the baby's father, he made his excuses to Oonagh and dashed out of the door, taking giant strides as he went. Finn MacCool threw off his baby disguise, leaped out of his cradle, and did a merry dance with Oonagh!

Benandonner, the Red Man, bounded all the way home to Scotland, kicking over the rocks in Finn MacCool's path as he went. Lucky MacCool was never tormented by the Scottish giant again—and it was all thanks to his clever wife, Oonagh, who had brains just as her husband had strength.

Theseus and the Minotaur

Of all the kings of Ancient Greece, King Minos of Crete was the most powerful, and he commanded an invincible army.

To keep him happy and to prevent him from waging war, all the other rulers sent gifts to him. Some gave him food and wine, some gave him silks and treasures, but every spring, King Aegeus of Athens was forced to send to King Minos seven young men and seven young women.

When they reached Crete, King Minos locked the poor young people in an impossible maze called a labyrinth, which was built beneath his palace. In the labyrinth lived a terrible raging monster called the Minotaur. The Minotaur had the body of a man, the head of a bull, and an appetite for humans. No person who entered the labyrinth ever came out alive.

In Athens, the time was approaching for King Aegeus to choose fourteen more youngsters to sacrifice to King Minos and his horrible Minotaur. However, this time, the king's son, Theseus, refused to accept such cruelty and unfairness.

"This isn't right, Father!" said Theseus. "You can no longer do this to your people. Let me go as a son of Athens, and I will slay this dreadful Minotaur!"

King Aegeus begged his son not to leave, but Theseus was brave and foolhardy, and his mind was made up. Soon, the prince set sail for Crete with thirteen other young Athenians.

When they arrived, they were greeted by a sneering King Minos and his daughter, Princess Ariadne. Minos taunted the Athenians and tutted, "Not much of a meal for my beast, are you? Such pathetic weaklings!"

When King Minos asked for their names, everybody cowered and stayed silent, except for Theseus, who stepped forward boldly. "I am Theseus, Prince of Athens, and I have come to slay your Minotaur!"

King Minos laughed. "Ha! Have you, now? Many before you have tried, and all have failed! You will die just as they did."

However, Princess Ariadne admired Theseus's courage and honesty, and she hated her father's cruelty. That night, she crept into the cell where Theseus and his fellow Athenians were chained up, and she woke him.

"Even if you kill the Minotaur, you will never escape from the labyrinth," she explained. She handed him a sword and a ball of thread. "Trail this thread behind you, and you will be sure to find your way out of the labyrinth."

Theseus thanked the princess for her great kindness.

"You can show me your thanks," she said, "by taking me with you when you leave—I cannot bear to live here a moment longer. Besides, my father will have me killed when he discovers what I have done."

If her plan was successful, Theseus vowed to help the princess escape.

At the break of dawn the next day, the king and his guards gathered to see Theseus and the other Athenians enter the labyrinth. The youngsters trembled with fear.

"Make sure he goes in first!" smiled King Minos, pointing at Theseus.

A guard grabbed the prince by the shoulder and shoved him roughly through the door of the labyrinth. It was pitch black inside, but for the faint flicker of burning torches.

The prince stood just inside the entrance, waiting for the other young people to be pushed inside, too.

"Stay here, and hold the end of this thread," he told them. "Whatever you do, don't let go of it. I will return for you as soon as I can!"

Theseus began to creep through the gloomy, confusing labyrinth, trailing the thread behind him as he went.

His path was littered with skeletons, and he walked into many dead ends. Sometimes, he spotted thread on the floor before him and knew that he had come full circle. He soon felt like he had walked for many hours.

When he finally stumbled upon the middle of the labyrinth, nothing could have prepared him for the monster he met there. The Minotaur's body was like a giant's, and his bullish head was as black as night, with flaming eyes and piercing horns.

When the Minotaur saw Theseus, it hunched its powerful shoulders and charged toward him at full speed, flinging the prince high into the air. Theseus landed with a bone-cracking thud. At that moment, he thought he would never survive, but then he remembered Princess Ariadne's sword, which was hidden beneath his tunic.

The Minotaur charged again, but this time, Theseus jumped to his feet and, quick as lightning, plunged the sword into the Minotaur's heart. It was enough to finish the mighty beast.

In the dim light, Theseus caught sight of the end of his thread trail and followed it back to his friends, who were overjoyed to see him.

With Theseus leading the way, the young Athenians escaped from the labyrinth to find an anxious Princess Ariadne waiting outside for them.

"You did it!" she exclaimed.

"But I would never have succeeded without your help," smiled Theseus.

Grabbing her hand, he dashed with the other Athenians toward the port, and they boarded their ship.

Before most of Crete had stirred from its sleep, the hero and his friends had sailed quietly away.

Even King Minos had gone back to bed, and fast asleep, he was quite unaware that his greatest weapon—the Minotaur—was lying dead in the labyrinth, and his days of tyranny were over.

The Boy Who Cried Wolf

Alfie was a shepherd boy, and it was his job, come rain or shine, to look after the sheep that belonged to his friends in the village.

One sunny day, he was sitting on the hillside watching the sheep, when he started to think about the younger children playing in the village. How he wished he could join them! Just remembering the fun he used to have made Alfie grow tired of his fleecy companions. He was bored with watching the clouds float by, and he'd climbed every tree.

"Wolf! Wolf! Help!"

"I wish something exciting would happen," he sighed. And then he had an idea—an idea filled with mischief.

Suddenly, Alfie shouted, "Wolf! Wolf! There is a wolf chasing the sheep!"

His cries were so loud that everyone in the village heard him, and they all came rushing up the hill with their hatchets to help drive the wolf away. But when they got there, there was no wolf to be found, and the sheep were lazily grazing on the grass, with not a care in the world. The boy chuckled to himself at the clever joke he had played on everyone.

"Tricked you!" he laughed, but the villagers weren't amused.

"What a foolish thing to do," they complained. "Never cry wolf unless there is truly a wolf to fear, Alfie." Then they went back to their business, leaving Alfie grinning on the hillside.

A few days later, Alfie was on the hillside and growing restless again—he had run out of ways to amuse himself.

"Time for a little more naughtiness," he thought, and he shouted, "Wolf! Wolf! Help! It's attacking the sheep!"

When the villagers heard his cries, they dashed up the hillside to protect their flock. But when they got there, there was not a wolf in sight!

"Tricked you again!" he giggled.

"Alfie!" scolded one of the villagers. "This isn't funny! You must never cry wolf unless there is truly a wolf!"

Feeling thoroughly cross with Alfie, they all headed back to the village, but he just shrugged—a little bit of mischief made his day less boring.

The next day, Alfie was on the hillside keeping an eye on the sheep, when he heard a rustle in the bushes.

The sheep started to bleat nervously and dart about, and a dark muzzle poked through the branches, baring sharp white teeth. It was followed by the bright flash of yellow eyes—they belonged to a wolf, and it was about to pounce on his sheep! Alfie was so scared, he ran into the bushes to hide.

"WOLF! WOLF!" he shouted, as the sheep scattered everywhere.

"WOLF! WOLF!" he shouted, as the wolf snapped at their tails. "Help! It's attacking the sheep!"

But this time when the villagers heard Alfie's cries, they just rolled their eyes and thought, "Oh, that's just Alfie, up to his old tricks again. He won't fool us this time!" And everybody ignored him and went about their business.

Later that day, just as the sun was setting, the villagers saw that Alfie hadn't yet returned with their sheep. A few of them wandered up the hillside to see why he was late, but when they got there, all they found were a few wispy strands of wool stuck to the thorny bushes.

"Alfie! Where are you?" they shouted.

The bushes parted, and out stepped Alfie, still shaking with fear.

"There really was a wolf this time," he sobbed. "Why did nobody help me?"

"Because we didn't believe you!" explained the eldest villager. "You tricked us twice before, and it's hard to know when a liar is telling the truth."

So, Alfie learned his lesson the hard way—nobody believes a liar, even if he is almost in the jaws of a wolf!

The Farmer's Horse

One wintry afternoon, a kind farmer was doing the rounds, feeding and checking on all his animals.

He decided to take his best sheepdog's new puppy with him, so that the little dog could get used to the strange sights, sounds, and smells of the farmyard. First, they checked on the sheep in the meadow. The frisky little pup barked with excitement when they greeted him with a chorus of baas, and he tried to herd them, just like he had seen his mother do.

Then they checked on the chickens, and the pup sniffed at them excitedly and wagged his tail—but he ran away whenever they pecked near his feet.

Next, they checked on the cows, and when they all gave a loud moo, the pup hid behind the farmer's legs, peeping out every now and then.

Finally, they came to the stables where the farmer kept his best-loved horse— she was a splendid chestnut-brown mare with a long, glossy mane. She would often carry the farmer to town, clip-clopping along the road, proudly swishing her silky mane.

The farmer fed the mare well and always gave her plenty of attention— more than any other farm animal.

When the farmer appeared with the excitable puppy at his heel, the mare wondered what this new little creature might be. The farmer patted the horse on the nose and said hello to the stable boy, who was busily moving hay with his pitchfork.

Then, rather than fussing over his mare as usual, the farmer sat down on a bale of hay. As soon as he did so, the playful little pup pranced and frisked around on his back legs, then ran circles around the farmer's feet.

The farmer and stable boy chuckled to see the puppy so excited, and they stroked behind his ears and patted his head. Enjoying the attention, the mischievous pup let out a high-pitched yap and jumped onto the farmer's lap, where the farmer fed him treats and stroked his tummy.

"So this is how I get all the attention now!" thought the farmer's horse, and she broke loose from her stable, reared onto her hind legs, and began to dance about just as she had seen the puppy do.

The farmer and stable boy doubled over with laughter at the sight, which encouraged the mare to dance and prance even more. Then, when the horse couldn't hold herself up any longer, she placed her hooves on the farmer's shoulders and tried to climb up onto his lap!

The little dog yelped, and fearing that the farmer and his new puppy would be crushed, the stable boy rushed over with his pitchfork and shouted at the horse to get down. The horse was led into her stable again and put in a harness. She didn't get any treats or fuss that night—and the farmer was very afraid to ride her.

That day, the farmer's horse learned that it's better to win the affection and admiration of others by being yourself, rather than by copying someone else.

St. George and the Dragon

St. George was a valiant knight who rode a magnificent horse as white as snow. He was famous far and wide for his bravery but, was about to face his greatest challenge.

Riding home from battle one day, St. George stopped to rest at a small market town, which was known for being a bright and bustling place. But on that day, it was eerily quiet—not a sound could be heard, and there was nobody to be seen. St. George wondered where everyone was.

An old man shuffled quietly out of the shadows and led St. George into a dark alley, where he told him of the terrible fate that had befallen the place. A fearsome dragon with fiery breath and leathery green scales had made its home in the nearby lake and was terrifying the whole area.

Nobody could slay the blood-curdling beast, so to stop it from burning their homes to the ground, the townsfolk offered their sheep and cattle to the hungry dragon. When these ran out, the king decreed that everybody in the kingdom—including the children—should place their names in a sack. Anyone whose name was drawn out was delivered to the dragon's watery home for its breakfast.

It greatly saddened the king to do this, as he was a good man at heart, but he didn't have the courage to face the dragon, and he could think of no other way to solve the problem.

And so, every two days, a name was drawn from the sack, and each time, the place grew a little sadder and a little quieter.

On the day that St. George arrived, the name of the king's own daughter had been drawn from the sack. Despite the king's protests, he had no choice but to be fair. The poor princess was taken to the dragon's lakeside lair and bound tightly to a tree. The people were about to lose their beloved princess, and there seemed to be no end to the dragon's reign of terror.

Courageous St. George was greatly angered when he heard the pitiful tale. He swiftly mounted his horse and galloped with great speed to the lake, where he found the princess.

As he drew near, he could see from her fearful expression that there was no time to cut her free—the dragon was close by. St. George turned just in time to see the horned back of the beast rear out of the lake. Its green scales glinted, and its dagger-sharp teeth flashed menacingly. Venomous smoke puffed from its nostrils, filling the air with a foul stench.

As the princess struggled desperately to free herself, St. George charged toward the dragon, armed with his trusty lance. The dragon snarled and spat out a searing jet of flames, narrowly missing the knight and his horse. With lightning reactions, St. George plunged his lance deep into the dragon's chest, and the beast fell to the ground with a helpless roar.

St. George quickly untied the princess and used the rope to tie a leash around the dragon's scaly neck. Together, the princess and St. George led the wounded dragon toward town.

When they reached the square, the brave knight summoned the king and all the townsfolk. He made the king vow in front of his people that he would never be so cowardly again and instead swear to protect the lives of his subjects. Overjoyed to see his daughter, the king agreed.

Then St. George killed the dragon, so that everyone knew they would no longer have to live in fear.

The king offered St. George all kinds of wonderful rewards for his heroism—jewels, gold, and a seat in his royal court—but St. George refused them all, claiming that the freedom of the people was reward enough.

He galloped away on his faithful white horse, leaving behind him the legend you read today.

The Dog and His Bone

Dog was having a lovely day in the park, nosing through the grasses, rolling in the daisies, and tracking down scents.

"Is there anything better than being a dog?" he thought to himself, as he sniffed his way through the long grass.

Just then, his nose caught a whiff of something interesting. Dog's head shot up, and he stayed completely still for a few seconds. He sniffed the air again—just to make sure—then he wagged his tail excitedly. Off he went at high speed, snuffling his way across the ground, following the scent trail. He was a dog on a very important mission.

Every now and then, Dog's head popped up, he sniffed again, his tail wagged, and off he went once more, hot on the trail! Suddenly, Dog stopped and dived his head deep into a clump of grass.

"Ooh, it can't be!" he thought. He took a long, deep sniff. "It is! It is!" and he wagged his tail even harder. Then Dog went straight to work—pawing away at the ground and digging up the soil with all his energy, until the scent was so strong, he snorted with excitement. One more swipe of paw, and there it was—a big white bone! Dog let out a happy little yelp.

"What luck! A nice, fat bone to gnaw on, and it's all mine!" said Dog, and he gripped it tightly in his mouth.

"Hmm, I'd better take this somewhere secret," he thought. "I don't want to share it with the other dogs!"

So off he scampered through the bushes and into the woods—all the time, clutching the bone between his teeth and looking from side to side to make sure no other dogs were following him.

Every so often, he'd hear the snap of a twig or the rustle of leaves, and Dog would stand still and growl, just in case another dog was about to pounce and snatch his bone away.

"I can't wait to gnaw on this nice, fat bone!" thought Dog. "I just need to find a safe spot where nobody can bother me." So on he went, farther into the woods.

At last, Dog came to a little stream with a little wooden bridge over it. On the other side was a patch of green grass—the perfect spot for gnawing bones!

But when Dog was halfway across the bridge, he saw something out of the corner of his eye. He looked down at the stream, and to his surprise, there was another dog holding a delicious-looking chewy bone in his mouth.

"Where did he come from?" thought Dog. "And how did he get a bone even bigger and better than mine?"

Dog snarled at the dog in the stream, but the dog in the stream just snarled back and kept on staring at him.

Dog growled at the dog in the stream, but the dog in the stream just growled back and didn't move an inch. "Right, I'll teach him!" thought Dog. "I'll grab his bone, too! Then I'll have two nice, fat bones to gnaw on!"

So Dog leaned over the edge of the bridge toward his rival and opened his jaws wide to snatch up the other dog's juicy bone. But as he opened his mouth, his own bone fell into the stream below him with a great splash. The ripples on the water made the other dog disappear.

Of course, there was no other dog in the stream at all—Dog had been looking at his own reflection all along, and thanks to his greed, he had lost his nice, fat bone!

Dog walked over the bridge, plumped himself down, rested his head on his paws, and let out a little whimper.

From this day on, he thought, I'll always be happy with what I've got!

The Four Harmonious Animals

One sizzling hot summer's day, an elephant was plodding along the riverbank looking for a spot to cool down in. After a while, he came to a wonderful tree with a big patch of shade beneath it.

It was a very special tree—its branches were long, its leaves were green and lush, and it was heavy with ripe, sweet fruit. Best of all, it provided enough shade to cool an elephant. Most pleased with himself, the elephant lay down to rest.

He had just made himself comfortable when a monkey appeared by his side, making quite a lot of noise.

"Oo-oo-oo! Excuse me, Elephant, but can you see any fruits hanging from the lower branches of this tree?"

The elephant looked at the branches above him. "No, I can't," he said.

"Well, that's because I ate those fruits long before you ever lay down in its shade. I saw this tree first, and it belongs to me!" said the monkey.

The elephant slowly lumbered to his feet. "I am sorry, friend. I didn't know this tree belonged to you. I was just enjoying its shade. I will move on."

But just as the elephant said this, a long-eared hare hopped by.

"What do you mean when you say this tree belongs to you, Monkey? I was nibbling at the leaves of this tree when it was just a tiny sapling. I think you'll find that this tree belongs to me!" said the hare.

Monkey looked at the hare and said, "We are sorry, friend. We didn't know this tree belonged to you. Elephant was just enjoying its cool shade, and I have been eating its delicious fruits. We will move on."

A flap of feathers from the top of the fruit tree caught the attention of all three animals. There sat a plump-looking partridge.

"What do you mean when you say that this tree belongs to you, Hare? This tree would not even exist if it weren't for me! I dropped the very seed that it grew from, so I knew this tree before any of you!"

The elephant, monkey, and hare all bowed deeply to the partridge, and the hare said, "We are sorry, friend. We didn't know this tree belonged to you. Elephant was just enjoying its cool shade, Monkey has been eating its delicious fruits, and I like to nibble on its leaves. We will move on."

The partridge looked thoughtful, then she flew down to the ground. She asked the three animals to stay.

"Since we all like this tree so much, why don't we share it?" suggested the partridge. "That way, we can all enjoy the tree—its cool shade, its sweet-smelling fruits, and its tender green leaves. And just wait until you smell its fragrant spring flowers!"

They agreed, and the four animals quickly became great friends. From that day on, they worked together as a team to enjoy their special tree.

The hare and the partridge worked in harmony to harvest the fruit on the ground and from the lower branches. The monkey climbed farther up the

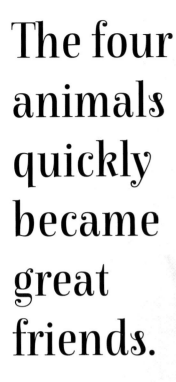

The four animals quickly became great friends.

tree to drop down the ripe fruits from the middle branches, and the elephant used his trunk to reach the fruit on the higher branches. Then they all sat together in the cool shade of the tree to enjoy their feast.

Sometimes, to reach the fruit right at the top, you would even see the partridge balancing on top of the hare's head, who was on the shoulders of the monkey, who was riding on the back of the elephant!

Thanks to their friendship and willingness to cooperate with each other, the four animals never went hungry or suffered in the heat again, and all around the forest, they became known as the four harmonious animals.

Pinocchio

By Carlo Collodi

How it came to pass that Mr. Cherry, the carpenter, found a piece of wood that laughed and cried like a child. There was once upon a time ...

"A king!" my little readers will instantly shout. No, children, you are mistaken. Once upon a time, there was a piece of wood. This wood was not the best, it was just a common log like those used in fireplaces to warm the rooms in winter.

How it came about I cannot tell, but the fact is that one day, this piece of wood just happened to be lying in the shop of an old carpenter whose real name was Mr. Antonio, but everyone called him Mr. Cherry because the end of his nose was always as red and shiny as a ripe cherry.

As soon as Mr. Cherry noticed this piece of wood, he was delighted. He rubbed his hands together with glee and said, "This has come at exactly the right time. It is just what I need to make a leg for my table."

He took his sharp hatchet to strip off the rough bark. But just as he was about to make the first strike, he stopped with his arm in the air, for he heard a very small voice begging him, "Don't strike me too hard!"

You can imagine Mr. Cherry's surprise. Terrified, he looked around the room to try to find where the tiny voice had come from, but he saw nobody! He looked under the bench—nobody. He looked in the cupboard, but there was nobody. He looked in the basket of sawdust—nobody. He opened the door of the shop and looked in the street—and still nobody.

"Oh, you hurt me!"

"I see how it is," he said, laughing. "I must have imagined that little voice. Now let's go to work!"

He picked up his hatchet and struck the piece of wood with a huge blow.

"Oh, you hurt me!" complained the same little voice.

This time, Mr. Cherry's eyes popped out of his head, his mouth was wide open, and his tongue hung out.

As soon as he could speak, he said, trembling and stuttering with fear, "Where on earth did that tiny voice come from that said 'Oh'? There's not a living soul here. Is it possible that this piece of wood has learned to cry like a child? I can't believe it. It's just a piece of firewood like all the others. Is someone hidden inside it? If there is, so much the worse for him!"

And he grabbed the poor piece of wood and, without mercy, started to beat it against the walls of the room.

Then he stopped and listened to see if he could hear the little voice crying out again. He waited two minutes—nothing; five minutes—nothing; ten minutes—and still nothing!

"I see how it is!" he said, forcing a laugh. "I must have imagined the voice. Let's get to work again." And, because he felt scared, he tried to sing to give himself some courage.

He began planing and polishing the piece of wood, but when the plane went up and down, he heard the same little voice say, laughing, "Stop! You're tickling me all over!"

This time, poor Mr. Cherry fell down as if struck by lightning. When he opened his eyes, he was on the floor. Even the end of his nose, which was always red, had turned blue with fright!

Just then, somebody knocked on the door. "Come in!" said the carpenter; but he had no strength to stand up.

A lively little old man walked into the shop. His name was Geppetto.

"Good morning, Mr. Antonio," said Geppetto. "What are you doing there on the floor?"

"I am teaching the alphabet to the ants. What has brought you here, Mr. Geppetto?"

"My legs. Mr. Antonio, I have come to ask something of you. I thought I would make a beautiful wooden puppet—a wonderful puppet that can dance, fence, and leap like an acrobat. With this puppet, I could travel the world. What do you think?"

"Well, Geppetto," said the carpenter, "what do you want from me?"

"I need a little piece of wood to make my puppet. Will you spare me some?"

Delighted, Mr. Antonio hurried to his bench and picked up the piece of wood that had frightened him so much. But just as he was giving it to his friend, it shook and wriggled out of his hands, and struck poor Geppetto on the shins.

Geppetto took the wood and, thanking Mr. Antonio, went limping home.

Geppetto's little room on the ground floor was lit by a window up the stairs. His furniture could not have been simpler—an old chair, a rickety bed, and a broken-down table. At one end of the room you could see a fireplace with the fire lit; but the fire was a painting. And by the fire was a painted kettle boiling cheerfully, with a cloud of steam just like real steam.

At home, Geppetto took out his tools and began to make his puppet.

"What shall I name him?" he thought. "I think I will call him Pinocchio—it is a name that will bring him luck.

Pinocchio

I once knew a family with this name. There was Pinocchio the father, Pinocchia the mother, and Pinocchii the children, and all of them did well. The richest of them was a beggar!"

Having found a name for his puppet, he set about to work. First, he made he puppet's hair, then his forehead, and then his eyes.

When the eyes were finished, imagine his astonishment when he saw them moving and staring at him! When Geppetto saw those wooden eyes staring at him, he did not like it, and he said angrily, "Naughty wooden eyes, why are you staring at me?"

No one answered.

So, then he started to carve the nose; but no sooner had he made it, than it began to grow. And it grew, and grew, and grew, until in a few minutes, it had grown so long that it seemed as if it would never end.

Poor Geppetto wore himself out trying to shorten it; but the more he cut off, the longer the impertinent nose grew!

After the nose, he made the mouth; but before he had even finished it, it began to laugh and poke fun at him.

"Stop laughing!" said Geppetto; but he might as well have been speaking to the wall.

"Stop laughing, I say!" he shouted.

The mouth stopped laughing and stuck out its tongue instead.

As Geppetto did not want to make a mess of his work, he pretended not to see it and continued carving.

After the mouth, he carved the chin, then the throat, then the shoulders, the stomach, the arms, and the hands.

Pinocchio's hands were barely finished when Geppetto felt his wig snatched from his head. He turned around, and what did he see? His wig in the puppet's hands!

"Pinocchio! Give me back my wig at once!"

But Pinocchio, instead of giving back the wig, put it on his own head and was almost completely covered by it.

This mischievous conduct made poor Geppetto feel sadder than he ever had before in his life.

He turned to Pinocchio and said, "You little rascal! You are not even finished, and you are already showing no respect for your father! That's bad, my boy, very bad!"

There were still the legs and feet to do. When Geppetto had finished the feet, he got a kick on the nose.

"It serves me right!" he said to himself. "I should have seen it coming. Now it is too late!"

"Pinocchio! Give me back my wig at once!"

Pinocchio

He then held the puppet under the arms and put him down on the floor to teach him to walk. Pinocchio's legs were stiff, and he couldn't move them, but Geppetto led him by the hand and showed him how to put one foot before the other.

When his legs felt less stiff, Pinocchio began to walk by himself and run around the room, until finally, he slipped out through the door and ran away!

Poor old Geppetto ran after him as quickly as he could, but he couldn't catch up, for the little rascal leaped in front of him like a hare, and his wooden feet on the pavement made as much clatter as twenty pairs of clogs. What happened afterward is almost too much to believe ...

Stone Soup

There was once an old wanderer who had walked many miles along the dusty road, and he was tired and hungry. On his back, he carried a large cauldron and a small knapsack, which seemed to grow heavier every second.

When he reached the next village, he was hoping that some kind person would offer him a bite to eat, but when he got there, he found that the villagers turned their faces away from him or hid behind their curtains and tutted—they certainly didn't welcome strangers begging at their door.

So the wanderer filled up his cauldron from the village well, made a small fire, and set the cauldron over it. He pulled a shiny stone out of his pocket and dropped it into the cauldron.

One of the villagers had been watching him and was curious, so she walked over to the wanderer.

"What are you making there, sir?" asked the villager.

"Stone soup!" said the wanderer.

"Stone soup?" puzzled the villager. "I've never heard of it!"

"Well, you're missing out!" smiled the wanderer. "My special stone makes the finest soup you've ever tasted. Amazing taste guaranteed!"

The wanderer sniffed at the cauldron of water with the stone in the bottom and licked his lips.

"Of course, stone soup with onion and carrots—now, that's even better!"

"I have an onion and some carrots!" said the villager, and she dashed off to get them.

She returned and the wanderer added the vegetables to the bubbling water. He sniffed at the soup again and gave a satisfied smile. Pretty soon, he was joined by a second curious villager.

"He's making stone soup!" explained the first villager with excitement.

"What's that?" asked the new arrival.

"It's the best soup ever! It has a special stone in it to add taste, you know," said the first villager.

"Indeed," said the wanderer, "it is the finest thing you'll ever eat. But, you know, stone soup with potatoes ... now, that's really special!"

The second villager didn't need to be persuaded. He dashed home to grab some potatoes and returned with them scrubbed and chopped. The wanderer threw them in his cauldron.

And so it went on. As the stone soup simmered away, more and more villagers came to see what smelled so good. It wasn't long before there was a crowd gathered around the wanderer's cauldron, all chatting about his miraculous soup stone.

And each time someone new came along, the wanderer suggested a new ingredient that would make his stone soup taste even finer. Soon, almost every person in the village had added something—mushrooms, herbs, salt, pepper, bacon, and chicken! One person brought bowls and spoons, and the baker brought bread rolls.

The villagers longed to taste the stone soup, and when it was ready, they all sat down on the village green to try it. After everyone had taken a mouthful, they all agreed that stone soup was indeed the greatest soup they had ever tasted, and they all thanked the wanderer for his kindness in sharing it with them. The baker even showed his gratitude by offering the wanderer a bed for the night.

When their bellies were full, the wanderer scooped the stone out of the cauldron and put it back in his pocket, then he smiled to himself, for it wasn't the stone that had made the soup great—it was the fact that everyone had worked together.

The Wooden Bowl

In the countryside of Japan, outside the great city of Kyoto, there lived an old couple with one daughter.

The old couple were poor but kind, and they raised their young daughter to work hard, be true, and have a good heart. The girl grew up to be as beautiful as a butterfly and as hard-working as an ox.

One day, her father passed away, and her mother became ill, too. The girl was weeping, and the old woman beckoned her and said, "Have I ever told you that you are as beautiful as a butterfly?"

"No, you haven't," said the girl, puzzled by her mother's question.

"Well, I worry that your beautiful face and gentle ways will cause people to take advantage of you. Please fetch me the great black rice bowl from the kitchen."

The girl did as she was told, and the old woman put it on the girl's head. "Now, all your beauty is hidden away from the world."

"But Mother, it's so heavy!" cried the girl.

"Promise me that you won't remove it until the time is right," said the old woman.

"But how will I know?" asked the girl.

"You will know," said the old woman, then she passed away with a peaceful smile.

The girl couldn't bear to stay in a place with such sad memories, so she tied up her belongings in a handkerchief and bravely set out to find a new life.

As she walked through the village, she knew what an odd sight she must be with a great black rice bowl covering her face. The villagers laughed and pointed as she passed by. Some of the children threw pebbles at her, and one man tried to remove the bowl, so he could see who was beneath it. But when he touched the bowl, it scalded his hand. He howled and ran away.

The girl continued on her way, passing through one village after the next asking for work. Each time it was the same—people just stared or laughed at her.

Eventually, the poor girl was so tired and hungry, she sat down by the road and cried. The tears rolled down her cheeks and dripped onto the ground.

Just then, a wandering minstrel passed by with a lute slung over his shoulder. "Girl with a black bowl on your head, why do you weep?" he asked.

"I weep because I am hungry, and nobody will give me work," she replied.

"I don't have a penny to spare, but I can sing you a song," said the singer, and he started to play a beautiful tune on his lute. He made up a song for the girl,

"The white cherry blooms by the roadside—under a heavy black cloud.

The white cherry droops by the roadside—under a heavy black cloud.

Hark, hear the rain, hear the rainfall!

Fall from a heavy black cloud."

The girl just kept on weeping, so the wandering minstrel went on his way and soon reached the house of a rich farmer. He knocked on the door and sang the same song for him.

"What does your song mean?" asked the farmer, so the minstrel told him that the white cherry was the face of a maiden he had just met, the black cloud was the black bowl on her head, and the rainfall was her tears.

"She said that she wept for hunger, because nobody would give her work," said the minstrel.

The farmer felt so sorry for the girl that he set out to find her and offered her a job harvesting his fields. The girl, who was as hard-working as an ox, harvested more than anyone else and soon became much loved by the farmer and his wife. When harvest time was over, they gave her work as a maid in their house. Though the girl was very happy, still the black bowl remained stuck on her head.

One weekend, the farmer's wife was anxious that the house should be tidy. "My son is coming home from Kyoto, and we are having many parties to celebrate," she explained.

The girl worked hard to make the house look lovely, and then she worked even harder in the kitchen to prepare drinks and food for the party.

When the son, who was a handsome young man, arrived later that day, the merrymaking began. By the evening, the guests called for more wine, so the son went into the kitchen to grab a bottle and was surprised to see a young girl with a great black rice bowl on her head, preparing food.

"Upon my life, I must see who is hiding under that black bowl!" he thought.

From that day on, the young man and girl spent every spare moment talking to each other. He found her to be good-hearted and gentle, and she thought the same of him. When it was time for him to return to Kyoto, he decided to stay on and ask the girl to marry him.

His parents threw their hands in the air—how could he marry a girl with a bowl on her head? But the young man had made up his mind.

"I love the girl with the great black rice bowl, and I will marry no other!"

And so the wedding date was set, and the farmer's wife and friends dressed the bride in a splendid white and gold kimono with a bright scarlet robe over the top.

"Now off with that bowl!" they all said, and they tugged at it as hard as they could, but the bowl would not budge. It was stuck fast.

"Please!" begged the girl. "You are giving me a headache!" and though she felt ashamed to marry wearing the black bowl, she stepped out for her ceremony.

When she reached the young man's side, they made their wedding vows, and he whispered in her ear, "I love you as you are—the great black rice bowl doesn't matter one bit to me."

At that very moment, there was a mighty crack, and the black bowl shattered into a thousand tiny pieces. As they showered to the ground, they became nuggets of silver and gold, shining pearls, and every precious jewel that you can imagine. The young bride and her wedding guests looked on in astonishment. but the groom only had eyes for his new bride. Smiling at her, he said,

"To see your face, at last, is more precious than any jewel."

Hans
the Rabbit Herder

Young Hans was a shepherd with a big heart and big ambitions, so when the Princess of Bavaria announced that she was holding a contest to find a suitor, Hans couldn't wait to enter.

On the morning of the contest, Hans and many excited young noblemen gathered in the castle grounds, where the king proclaimed, "The princess will marry whoever catches this golden apple and completes two impossible challenges!"

With that, the princess tossed the golden apple high into the air. However, just at that moment, the sun came out and shone brightly into the eyes of her hopeful suitors.

Everyone covered their eyes except for Hans, who was used to bright sunshine from his days spent herding sheep on the hillsides. He leaped into the air and grabbed the golden apple before it hit the ground.

"Can you spare a little bread for an old man?" asked the beggar.

"Sure," smiled Hans. "Help yourself."

The old man ate the bread and asked Hans why he looked so downhearted. Hans explained his dilemma.

"Well," said the old man, "in return for your kindness, I'll give you something that may help." He handed Hans a small flute. "Just blow on it," explained the beggar, "and you will see." Then he shuffled away.

When the royal family saw that a lad in peasant's clothes had caught the apple, they were distraught. But the king had to be fair—he had no choice but to give Hans his first challenge.

"Tomorrow at dawn, I will release one hundred rabbits into the wild. You must bring them back to me in the evening."

Hans agreed, but he felt doomed to fail—rabbits were much more difficult to herd than sheep. He walked home in a gloomy mood and, along the way, sat down to eat a crust of bread and think about his challenge. As he was eating, an old beggar passed by.

The next day, feeling in better spirits, Hans arrived at the castle. "I'm here to herd your rabbits!" he told the king.

The king released the hundred rabbits, and they hopped about, instantly scattering all over the fields. Soon, only a few of them could be seen.

Hans walked across a large field and sat down by a tree. He took out his flute, and hiding it under his tunic, he blew on it. Within minutes, one hundred rabbits were by his side!

The king, queen, and princess were spying on Hans from the castle, and when they saw the rabbits bounce back to him, they were most unhappy.

The princess could never marry a lowly shepherd! Together, the royal family thought of a plan to make sure that Hans failed his challenge.

The princess, disguised as a kitchen maid, walked across the field to Hans.

"Oh, your rabbits are so adorable!" she cried. "Please will you sell one to me? I have always wanted a pet!"

But Hans was no fool. He immediately saw that it was the princess.

"They're not for sale," he said. "But you can earn one by giving me a kiss!"

The princess gasped with horror. A royal could never do such a thing! But then she remembered that she was a royal in disguise.

"Take it or leave it," shrugged Hans.

The princess was so determined to see Hans fail, she gave him a kiss. And in return, he gave her a rabbit. However, as soon as the princess reached the castle gates, Hans blew on his flute, and the rabbit hopped out of her basket and back to his side.

Too ashamed to admit to their kiss, the princess told the queen that Hans had stubbornly refused to sell her a rabbit.

"Let me try!" cried the queen, and she set off from the castle disguised as a washerwoman. She waddled up to Hans and asked, "Are these your rabbits? Can I buy one for my granddaughter, please?"

"They're not for sale," he said, seeing immediately that it was the queen in disguise. "But you can earn one by rubbing my aching feet!"

The queen was disgusted. How could she—a royal!—rub a shepherd's feet?

However, she was desperate for the princess to marry someone better than Hans, so she rubbed his feet, and in return, he gave her a rabbit. But just as she reached the castle gates, Hans blew on his flute, and the rabbit wriggled out of her arms and hopped back in his direction.

Too embarrassed to admit that she had rubbed a shepherd's feet, the queen told the king that Hans could not be persuaded to sell his rabbits.

"I'll settle this!" cried the king, and he disguised himself as a woodcutter, trailing a donkey behind him.

"Good day, young man," he said to Hans. "Are these your rabbits? I'd like to buy one for my dinner."

"Oh, they're not for sale," said Hans, who knew the king instantly. "But I'll give one to you if you go and kiss your donkey!"

The king's made a fine face! "How dare he!" thought the king, but he was so desperate for Hans to fail, that he closed his eyes, puckered up his lips, and gave the donkey a great big kiss! Hans tried not to laugh as he handed a rabbit to the king.

The flustered king walked back to the castle. But when he reached the gates, Hans blew on his flute, and the rabbit bounded back to him.

"You were both right," said the red-faced king to the queen and princess. "What a stubborn fellow he is!"

So, as the sun began to set, Hans strolled back to the castle with all one hundred rabbits at his side.

"Well done," grumbled the king. "Come back in the morning for your final task."

The royal family stayed up all night trying to come up with an impossible challenge for Hans.

The next morning, Hans was ushered into the castle's great hall. With a sly smile, the king announced, "This last challenge is simple—just sing these three bags full." Then a guard placed three empty bags before Hans.

"No problem!" smiled Hans. "But I'd love to have an audience for my singing. Why not invite the lords and ladies of your court to see it?"

The king agreed, and soon the great hall was teeming with people who had come to witness the spectacle of Hans singing the empty bags full.

When everybody was ready, Hans stood before the first bag and sang,

"Our princess, dressed in disguise
As a pretty miss,
She tried to win a rabbit,
In return, I won a ..."

"Stop!" cried the princess, with cheeks burning red. "I declare the bag is full! That bag is quite full!"

Of course, the bag was empty, but the princess didn't want Hans to complete his song and reveal that she had kissed him.

Hans bowed low before her and moved on to the second bag.

He began to sing,

"Our queen, she dressed in disguise
As a washerwoman neat,
She tried to win a rabbit
By rubbing my aching ..."

"Enough!" squealed the queen in horror. "The bag is full! The bag is full!"

Hans smiled, bowed low, and walked up to the last empty bag. He took a deep breath and sang,

"Our king, he dressed in disguise,
With a donkey at his hips,
To try to win a rabbit,
He kissed a donkey on the ..."

"Bravo!" shouted the king. "Well done—the last bag is full!"

There was nothing the royal family could do! Hans, the lowly shepherd, had outwitted them all, and he married the princess that very day.

Everyone in the great hall attended, and a grand time was had by all— especially the hundred rabbits, which Hans summoned with his magic flute.

The Fox and the Crow

Mrs. Crow was flying over a garden one day, when she spotted a delicious chunk of cheese lying on the lawn. She swooped down, grabbed it with her beak, and flew over to a big oak tree with a wide branch—just right for perching on and having a bite to eat.

She made herself comfortable and was just about to nibble at the cheese, when a squirrel scurried up the tree trunk toward her.

"Oh, hello Mrs. Crow! What a fine feast you have before you!" he said. "I, myself, haven't eaten today. Perhaps you would be good enough to share it with me?"

"Oh no!" said Mrs. Crow. "This is my cheese! I found it, and I'm going to gobble it all up!"

Then she pushed the cheese under her feathery tummy and gave the squirrel a stern look with her beady crow eyes.

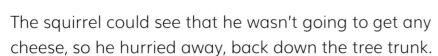

The squirrel could see that he wasn't going to get any cheese, so he hurried away, back down the tree trunk.

"Phew!" thought Mrs. Crow. "Now I can enjoy my cheese."

She was about to take a big, satisfying peck, when she heard a yappy bark from down below. At the bottom of the tree was a little puppy, jumping up the tree trunk and scratching it excitedly with her paws.

"Is that cheese you've got, Mrs. Crow?" woofed the pup. "Oh, I love cheese! Can I have some please?" Then she yapped at the thought of a cheesy feast.

"Oh no!" said Mrs. Crow. "This is my cheese! I found it, and I'm going to gobble it all up!"

Then she spread out her wings to make herself look big and scary. The little pup knew she was out of luck, so she ran off, looking for a ball to play with.

"Thank goodness for that," thought Mrs. Crow. "Now I can enjoy my cheese."

Her beak was just about to sink into the delicious chunk, when she heard a cluck-cluck-clucking and a chirp-chirp-chirping under the tree. She looked down, wondering what the noise was. It was a hen and her fluffy chicks.

"Ooh, cheese!" said the hen. "I love it! Mrs. Crow, please could you spare some cheese for my hungry chicks?"

"Oh no!" said Mrs. Crow. "This is my cheese! I found it, and I'm going to gobble it all up!"

Then she let out an almighty "Caaaw!" to scare the hen and her chicks away. It worked—they went strutting back to the henhouse, flapping their feathers and clucking all the way.

"Finally!" sighed Mrs. Crow. "Now I can enjoy my lovely cheese without any more interruptions."

She lifted up the cheese in her beak and was just about to swallow it, when she heard a charming voice at the bottom of the tree. She looked down to see a fox leaning on the tree trunk.

"It can't be! Yes, it is. I thought so!" said the fox. "Mrs. Crow—the queen of birds! I heard that wonderful 'Caw' just now, and I knew it must be you!"

Mrs. Crow was enjoying the fox's flattering words.

"How well you look today," he said. "Are your feathers even glossier than usual? Are your eyes even brighter?"

Mrs. Crow's beady eyes twinkled with delight at his compliments.

"Please give me just one more song in that beautiful voice of yours," begged the fox. "I hate to ask, but it would make me so happy."

Mrs. Crow fluffed up her feathers with pride, opened her beak, and let out a screeching "Caaaaaaw!". Of course, the cheese tumbled from her beak and fell straight into the fox's mouth.

The fox darted away with a full tummy, and Mrs. Crow sat on the branch without her cheese, regretting that she had ever been vain enough to be fooled by the fox's flattery.

The Wise Folk of Gotham

When the good people of Gotham in Nottinghamshire heard that King John was planning to build a hunting lodge in their village, they were most unhappy.

Not only did the king have a reputation for being a tyrant and an expensive guest to look after, he would most certainly steal their land for hunting and call it his own. Determined to keep their village and their hard-earned money for themselves, the Gotham folk got together and came up with a plan—a plan to make the king's messengers flee and, hopefully, tell King John to stay away.

When two of the king's messengers arrived the following week, they were surprised to see many of the villagers standing around a wooden fence in the village square, looking woeful.

"What on earth is going on here?" asked a messenger.

"It's such a pity," sobbed one lady. "We love the cuckoo's song so much, we decided to catch one and keep it in the middle of the village. We built a fence around it, so it couldn't fly away."

"We wanted to hear it sing every day," sighed the man standing next to her. "But when we got up this morning, we found that the cuckoo had flown away!"

"We should have built a higher fence!" said the lady. And with tears in their eyes, the villagers shook their heads sadly and walked away.

The messengers looked at each other in disbelief and laughed at the foolishness of the villagers.

They headed toward the local inn, which was across a small bridge, just outside the village. When they got to the bridge, they found two men fishing from the stream below.

"Caught anything yet?" asked one of the messengers.

"Nothing all day but this giant eel!" cried one of the fishermen. "We think it must have eaten up all the fish."

"We're just deciding how to punish it," explained the other fisherman. "We thought about chopping it up, but we've decided to drown it instead!"

And with that, his friend threw the big eel back into the stream below, and it quickly wriggled away. The king's messengers raised their eyebrows and continued on toward the inn.

After they had tied up their horses, they met a man who was much too big for the horse he was sitting on— and laid across the horse's back were two heavy sacks.

"Don't you think your horse is a little small to carry such a huge burden?" said one messenger, quite alarmed at the sight. "Why don't you get off and lead your horse?"

"I can't walk ... I've hurt my foot, sir, but you're right," said the man, then he thought for a while.

He took the two sacks and heaved one over each shoulder. "There!" he said. "Now I'm sharing the load with my horse." And off he trotted, with his poor horse panting all the way.

The two messengers looked at each other and rolled their eyes.

As they reached the entrance to the inn, they found the owner chatting to a brown hare.

"If you'll just give me a moment, sirs," explained the innkeeper. "I have to send my rent to my landlord in York, since I'm too busy to ride there. I thought if I caught a hare and sent it, it would be easier. There's nothing quicker than a hare, after all!"

The innkeeper tied a purse around the hare's neck and said, "Be sure to go straight there. Don't forget: straight road to Nottingham, then on to York. He lives by York cathedral. Someone will give you directions."

He patted the hare on the head and said, "Off you go!" and the hare ran off in the opposite direction.

"He must know a shortcut," shrugged the innkeeper, and he smiled.

By now the two messengers had truly had enough of the silliness of Gotham's good people.

"Good grief! The king cannot be seen in the company of such fools!" whispered one messenger to the other.

The other messenger didn't need to be persuaded. "We must return to his court with great haste and make sure he changes the location of his hunting lodge. They're all idiots!"

The king's messengers mounted their horses and sped away from Gotham, never to be seen again. As they left, the big man got off his tiny horse and winked at the innkeeper, the two fishermen patted each other on the back, and the villagers around the cuckoo fence laughed.

Their cunning plan had worked—and Gotham was forever safe from the hands of cruel King John.